ON A CANADIAN DAY

Nine Story Voyages Through History

Rona Arato

Illustrated by Peter Ferguson

MAPLE
TREE
PRESS

Maple Tree Press books are published by Owlkids Books Inc.
10 Lower Spadina Avenue, Suite 400, Toronto, Ontario M5V 2Z2
www.owlkids.com

Distributed in Canada by Raincoast Books
9050 Shaughnessy Street, Vancouver, British Columbia V6P 6E5

Distributed in the United States by Publishers Group West
1700 Fourth Street, Berkeley, California 94710

Library and Archives Canada Cataloguing in Publication

Arato, Rona
     On a Canadian day : nine story voyages through
history / Rona Arato ; illustrated by Peter Ferguson.

ISBN 978-1-897349-50-2 (bound).--ISBN 978-1-897349-51-9 (pbk.)

     1. Canada--History--Juvenile fiction.
I. Ferguson, Peter, 1968- II. Title.

PS8601.R35O5 2009   jC813'.6   C2009-901002-X

Library of Congress Control Number: 2009923328

Design: Susan Sinclair/Celeste Gagnon

Canada Council   Conseil des Arts   ONTARIO ARTS COUNCIL
for the Arts   du Canada   CONSEIL DES ARTS DE L'ONTARIO

We acknowledge the financial support of the Canada Council for the Arts, the Ontario Arts Council, the Government of Canada through the Book Publishing Industry Development Program (BPIDP), and the Government of Ontario through the Ontario Media Development Corporation's Book Initiative for our publishing activities.

Printed in China

A   B   C   D   E   F

Dear Reader,

The land we today call Canada has been home to people for thousands of years. For over four hundred years, people have come from all over the world to make this place their home as well. Some came seeking adventure, others were looking to make money. Most came looking for better lives in a free country. And all of them have a story.

Welcome to *On a Canadian Day*. In this book you will meet nine twelve-year-old kids at different times in Canadian history. Although these children aren't real, their lives and experiences are based on real events and the customs of their time. So turn the page to meet these kids—their experiences may be different, but their feelings are often like your own.

Rona Arato

The Buffalo Hunt

The Great Plains, 1620

Morning

Little Wolf opened his eyes. It was dark inside the tipi but he could tell from the birdsong that dawn was breaking in the eastern sky. Sliding out from between the two buffalo hides that were his bed, he crept from the tipi. Soon his family would be awake. He wanted these few minutes to himself.

It was the morning of his first buffalo hunt with the men of his camp. This day was a big moment in any young man's life, and that made him excited—and more than a little bit nervous. He crossed the camp in search of a quiet place.

Already people were stirring. He nodded to his grandmother, whose grey head was bent over the fire she was kindling. She was the oldest woman in the camp and had lived for over seventy winters.

"Good morning, Little Wolf," she smiled, exposing a gap where her front teeth had been. "Today you will go on your first buffalo hunt." Her black eyes examined him from a nest of wrinkles. "I hope you will find meat for my cooking pot."

He smiled back. "For you, I will find enough meat for ten cooking pots."

His grandmother chuckled and nodded as she turned back to her fire.

Little Wolf entered the grove of trees at the edge of the camp. Away from prying eyes, he sat down and pulled out his medicine bundle. He opened the

On a Canadian Day

pouch and poured the contents into his hand: a large pebble shaped like a bird's egg, a two-pronged tree branch, and a handful of dried pumpkin seeds. These objects reminded him of the bond his people shared with everything on the Earth. Closing his eyes, he prayed to the spirits to make his first hunt a success.

"Little Wolf, there you are."

Little Wolf jumped at the sound of his sister's voice.

"Father is looking for you. The men are preparing to leave for the hunt."

Little Wolf rose to his feet. "They won't leave without me."

"They will if you don't hurry." She placed her hands on her hips and looked him up and down. "If it were my first hunt, I would be ready with my arrows, not sitting under a tree dreaming."

"You can't hunt. You're a girl." Little Wolf pulled himself to his full height, which was half a head taller than his sister. He was twelve winters old; she was ten. Her black hair hung in two long braids to her shoulders. Her simple leather dress was belted at the waist and her feet were bare. His sister always wanted to do what he did, but he was a boy, born to hunt, while she was meant to stay home and watch after the camp. Besides, he could not imagine his sister hurting an animal. For a moment, he wondered if even he would be able to harm such a big living thing. He put the thought aside. He was a man: hunting was his job.

"Little Wolf, come." His sister stamped her foot.

"Yes, Sister." Little Wolf laughed and followed her back to the camp.

Their father was waiting in front of the family's tipi.

"This is not a day for you to wander off," he said, fixing Little Wolf with a stern gaze. **"Get your robe and your bow and arrows."**

His father was the son of a chief and held himself with a stern authority. When he spoke, everyone paid attention. He was dressed much the same as Little Wolf. Because the weather was warm his chest was bare. A soft leather strip called a breechcloth was tucked between his legs and draped over a belt. Two leather panels tied to the belt hung down the front and back of his legs. His black hair was tied into two long braids topped with an eagle feather. He looked down at Little Wolf and handed him a strip of dried buffalo meat. "Eat this for strength."

As Little Wolf bit off a piece, he thought of the tremendous effort that had gone into planning today's hunt. First a council of respected elders had met to choose men who were responsible for finding a herd—quite a task as it had been many moons since the camp had last seen a buffalo herd. Once they found one, they reported back to the camp. The hunters then prepared to follow the buffalo and guide them to the hunt site. And today, he was one of those hunters.

His mother looked at him with pride. "Good luck, my son. Your buffalo will fill our cooking pot."

"I will kill the biggest buffalo you have ever seen." Little Wolf held his arms out as far as they would go.

His sister tilted her head to one side. Her eyes danced with mischief. "And will you kill this huge buffalo all by yourself?"

Their father frowned. "Do not tease the spirits," he told his daughter. "We will catch what they allow." He put his hands on his son's shoulders. "For many seasons you have practiced being a part of the hunt. Today you will test your bravery and your skill. Only then will you become a man."

Afternoon

The sun had climbed halfway up the sky by the time the men reached the hunting ground. Little Wolf stood next to his father's younger brother. His uncle was as strong and imposing as a bear, but he also had a softer side. He liked playing with the children and telling stories around the campfire at night.

"Come here, Nephew," said his uncle. "The buffalo are in this direction." He pointed across the plain toward a small hill. "How should we approach them?"

"We must be very quiet so the buffalo will not know we are near," said Little Wolf, hoping he was right.

"Yes," said his uncle, "but there is more. What can you tell me about the wind?"

Little Wolf looked again where his uncle had pointed. A soft breeze blew into his face.

"That it is coming from the same direction, from where the buffalo are?" offered Little Wolf.

"That is right," said his uncle. "We are downwind of the buffalo, and that is how it must be for our hunt to succeed. The buffalo have an excellent sense of smell. If the wind was blowing from where *we* are toward the herd, our scent would be carried right to them." He made a gesture with his hand. "They would know we were coming, and before we could even see them, the whole herd would be gone."

Little Wolf nodded. He had heard tales of hunts where the buffalo ran off so fast the hunters came back empty-handed. But today they could not let that happen. It had been too long since the last hunt. His camp depended on the buffalo for food, clothing, and shelter—for their very lives.

"Come." His uncle put a finger to his lips, reminding Little Wolf to be quiet. At first, Little Wolf couldn't see much reason to stay quiet. The buffalo were very far away. He shaded his eyes. It was hot today, especially under the sun. A fly landed on his nose. He was brushing it away when he heard it—the thunder of hundreds of buffalo hooves pounding the ground. He drew in his breath.

The buffalo runners—the men who were luring the herd in their direction—were close now. These young men understood the ways of the animals. They got the herd to follow them by imitating the cries of a lost calf. Sometimes they wore animal skins to blend in with the buffalo. As the men moved forward, the herd followed. Little Wolf could see them now, and the enormity of their task became clear. His group of hunters aimed to drive these huge shaggy animals off a cliff, killing every one of them. But the herd—a massive bulge of brown fur—was vast. So many buffalo to control…

"Little Wolf!" his father hissed sharply. "Come, it is time."

His father led his group of hunters carefully in behind the herd, as the buffalo runners guided the animals between two lines of stone cairns, or walls. These cairns had been used for hundreds of years to lead buffalo toward a steep cliff. Once they were inside, the hunters would frighten the animals from behind to panic them into a stampede. Today, they did the same as the herd galloped into a tight column within the walls. "Wait," his father cautioned. "We do not want them to stampede until the last possible moment."

The hunters followed carefully behind the herd as it moved closer and closer to the edge. Little Wolf clutched his robe tightly in his sweating hands. This was what he would use to help urge the buffalo into a full stampede. His quiver full of arrows was slung over his shoulder. Looking at the huge animals, he hoped he wouldn't need them. His uncle came up beside him.

"Remember, young one," he whispered, "these animals are very dangerous when frightened. When we start the stampede stay alert and out of their way!" Little Wolf swallowed hard and looked up at his uncle, who flashed a smile, then turned his full attention to the giant herd. It was time.

"Now!" his father cried.

The hunters closed in on the herd, circling behind them and waving their robes to frighten the animals. Panic began to spread through the buffalo and the stampede was on. Little Wolf's heart raced as the deafening sound of their hooves grew even louder. He felt the ground shake as the giant beasts ran toward the cliff. The lead buffalo were almost at the edge when, sensing danger, they dug their heels into the rocky soil, sending up a spray of dust and stones. But it was too late. From behind came the unstoppable force of dozens of terrified animals. Little Wolf watched in amazement as the entire herd streamed forward like a raging river. It flowed between the stone cairns and then, in a giant rush of fur and kicking hooves, tumbled over the cliff into the valley below.

"Little Wolf," said his father as he strode up to him, "you did well, Son."

Little Wolf opened his mouth but no words came out. He was stunned, rooted to the spot by the spectacle he had just witnessed.

"Yes, he did do well," agreed his uncle, pointing down over the edge. "But the work is not finished."

Little Wolf followed his uncle's hand and looked down into the valley where an entire herd of dead and injured buffalo was piled against the cliff. Members of his camp who had been waiting below were busy killing the surviving animals.

"Wounded buffalo are still very dangerous," said his father. "We must go down and help. Ready your bow and arrows!"

Little Wolf followed the hunters to a safe path down the cliff. As he got closer, the animals that had looked so small from above became large again. Two hunters raced in front of him, chasing down a huge buffalo that had amazingly survived the fall by landing and rolling down the pile of animals. Little Wolf drew his bow and stayed close to his father.

Suddenly, a deeply wounded bull stumbled toward them. Despite his injuries, his determination made him strong—and fast. "Little Wolf!" cried his father. "Your arrows!"

As Little Wolf readied an arrow, his father drew back his bow and shot. The arrow grazed the animal's thick hide harmlessly. The bull kept coming.

Little Wolf steadied himself as he was taught to do. *No time to panic*, he thought. As he pulled back on his bow, he stared into the deep brown eyes of the bull. He saw that it was scared. He was scared, too. But without the meat and hide of the buffalo, his people could not live. This was his moment to prove his worth. He shouted as he let the arrow fly. It whistled through the air, driving deep into the bull's chest. The animal tumbled to the ground in a burst of dust. The bull's breathing slowed and the animal stopped moving.

"Little Wolf!" shouted his uncle. "Excellent shot, boy!"

Little Wolf's skin tingled and beads of moisture trickled down his cheeks. He wiped his face with his arm. Around him the noise and confusion of the hunt was dying down. In the distance, he saw the rest of the camp approaching. His mother and sister were with the women. The hunt was over. Now the butchering was to begin.

Evening

A large temporary camp had been set up on a vast field at the base of the cliff. With the hunting done, the women took over, cutting up and butchering the buffalo. They skinned the animals and then cut up the meat. Some of it would be cooked and eaten fresh. The rest was cut into thin strips that were hung on clean wooden poles. Over the next few days they would be smoked and then dried in the sun. Dried meat was lighter to carry than fresh meat and lasted a long time. It provided the camp with food during times when the buffalo were scarce.

Little Wolf knew that the women would be busy all night. It was important that the meat was prepared before it had a chance to spoil. Then they would render the animal fat into grease that could be stored for later use and extract marrow from the bones. Suddenly Little Wolf was starving. His mouth was dry and filled with dust from the hunt. He had not eaten or drunk anything since the morning. He walked over to where his mother and sister were sitting.

"So now you are a great buffalo hunter," his sister said, looking up from the buffalo hide she was scraping clean.

"Yes." Little Wolf puffed out his chest.

"And a hungry one, I'll bet," said his mother. She motioned for him to follow her to the cooking fire the women had made in the centre of the camp.

"Here." His mother filled a buffalo horn from a previous hunt with water from a large skin container.

Little Wolf drank deeply and then accepted a chunk of roasted meat from his grandmother. "I kept my promise," he said as he took a bite.

"You have filled my cooking pot well," she laughed.

"And you fill my stomach," he smiled. Walking back to his mother he looked up. The black bowl of sky was studded with tiny points of light. He yawned as his uncle approached him.

"And so, my young man, how does it feel to be a great hunter?"

"It feels good, Uncle. Next time I would like to hunt for antelope." He pantomimed shooting with his bow and arrow.

His uncle threw back his head and laughed. "These old bones can stalk the buffalo, but it takes strong young legs like yours to race after antelope."

Little Wolf bid his uncle good night and went to the spot where his family's buffalo hides were set out in a circle.

"It has been a long day," his father said as he sank onto his robe. "We must all get some rest."

"So tell me. Do you still want to be a buffalo hunter?" Little Wolf asked his sister, as she settled beside him.

"No," she laughed. "I will let you chase the animals while I turn them into food."

Little Wolf lay on his back and folded his arms beneath his head. The orange ball of the moon had risen, casting a pale light over the vast plain. He saw people working. Others had disappeared into tents or, like his family, were sleeping out in the open. He wanted to stay awake; to keep this amazing day from ending. But his lids were getting heavy.

A few minutes later, his father's soft snores drifted into the air, but for Little Wolf, sleep would not come. Every time he closed his eyes, he saw the face of the buffalo he had killed. It was as though the animal's spirit was calling out to him.

"Forgive me," Little Wolf whispered into the night air. "I would not kill you but to feed my family."

The buffalo looked at him once more and then closed its eyes. "My spirit is at peace," it seemed to say.

My spirit, too, is at peace, Little Wolf thought. Tomorrow, he decided, he would add one of the buffalo's teeth to his medicine bundle. That way his spirit would forever be linked to that of the animal of his first hunt.

This time when he closed his eyes, he drifted into a deep sleep in which hundreds of buffalo rumbled across the land and he was the chosen hunter who would lead them to the jump.

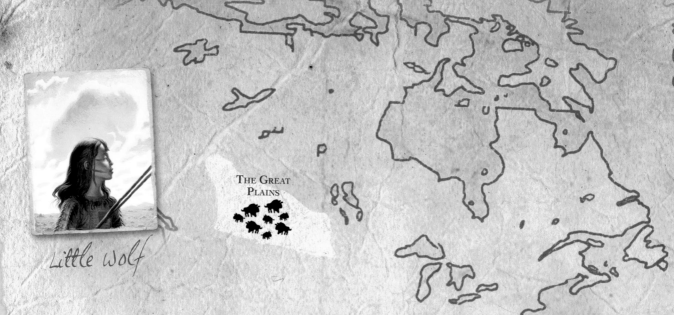

Little Wolf

THE GREAT
PLAINS

A Part of the Land:
Plains Aboriginal People

For thousands of years,
my people have lived in the Great Plains,
which includes the Canadian prairie
provinces of Alberta, Manitoba, and
Saskatchewan and American Midwestern
states such as Kansas and Oklahoma.
There are over thirty Aboriginal nations
on the Plains, including the Blackfeet,
Cree, Sioux, Crow, Cheyenne, and
Commanche. While our lifestyles are
similar, each nation has its own distinct
language, culture, and clothing.

Life on the Plains is difficult. Our winters
are long and cold and the summers
hot and dry. There is little natural
vegetation, and our people rely on the
buffalo for most of our needs. We kill
only as many as we need and use every
part of the animals we do kill.

Tipis are often decorated
with patterns or pictures.

After the men bring home the buffalo, our women scrape the inside of the hides free of fat and leave them outside to dry. Once the hides are cured they become blankets, robes, gloves, and costumes for ceremonies and hunting. Some hides are scraped free of hair. We use these for ropes, shields, clothing, pouches, and tipi covers.

We have many other uses for the buffalo. We use sinew as string, while the bones become tools. The horns make excellent spoons, cups, and bowls for eating. The tail and beard are used for decorations on clothing and weapons. Hooves are boiled to make glue and the buffalo's fat becomes hair grease, soap, and candles. We use the stomach for a cooking pot and the bladder as a pouch to carry tools or water.

Some Aboriginals are nomadic. They move from one place to another following the buffalo. They trade the meat and hides for vegetables grown by semi-nomadic nations. Semi-nomadic people, like my tribe, live in villages and go on hunting trips.

For thousands of years, our only domesticated animal has been the dog. We live near rivers or other water sources. When we travel, it is on foot. Our dogs help us carry supplies. We strap tent poles to their shoulders and tie supplies to these poles. Travelling this way is very slow, so we don't usually go long distances.

These are just some of the things we make using materials from the buffalo.

Hunters use robes to frighten a buffalo herd into a stampede. It's a scary time!

A New Life for Henri

New France, 1685

Henri Bernier pulled off his mittens and rubbed his hands together to get the circulation going. The weather had turned bitterly cold overnight, and his fingers and toes were numb. Papa had told him that the opportunities they enjoyed by living in New France made it worth putting up with the terrible weather. But sometimes Henri wished they were in Marseilles, where his mother had been born.

He had loved listening to her stories about that city's bright sunshine and soft warm air, even in the winter. But in France, Mama had been a poor servant girl with no hope to ever marry. So she had come to New France as one of the "King's Daughters"—*filles du roi*—women who were shipped across the ocean to marry men in Québec. That's how she met Papa.

When he thought of Mama, Henri's eyes filled with tears. She died last year giving birth to Henri's baby sister, Jacqueline, the fourth Bernier child. So much had changed since then. Now Papa was married to Charlotte, the daughter of a neighbouring farmer, and Henri was going to Québec City as an apprentice carpenter to his uncle Pierre.

Henri pulled his mittens back on and stamped his feet, which were going numb from the cold. He had better hurry and feed the pigs. Charlotte did not like it when he was late for breakfast. And today was his last morning at home. *It would not do to get her angry*, he thought as he gripped the slop bucket. He had done that too often.

The frozen ground was as hard as the rocks he and Papa had yanked out of the ground to create their fields. In France, Papa had been a poor man who was looking for adventure and a brand-new start to his life. So he came to New France as an *engagé*, or indentured servant. That meant that for a small salary and a place to live, he would spend three years helping to clear land and erect buildings throughout the colony.

For a long time, Papa thought he would become a fur trader after his three years as an *engagé* were complete. But he fell in love with life on the farm and started one of his own.

Henri reached the enclosure where the family's two pigs were rooting. It was late March but still there was no sign of spring. Frigid winds swept down from the north to coat the ground with frost.

"Bonjour," he said to the sow that waddled over and stuck her nose through the fence outside the barn. "You must be hungry." The sow snorted while a boar ignored his presence and rooted for food. Henri hoisted the bucket over the fence and filled the pigs' trough. She lowered her head and slurped greedily as the boar slowly lumbered over to get his breakfast.

Next, Henri walked into the barn, inhaling its comforting smell of dried hay and chicken feathers. Mimi, the family horse, lifted her head when he entered. Her soft brown eyes followed him as he filled her feed bag with oats. *"Bonjour,* Mimi," Henri said as he attached the bag to her harness. The horse whinnied her thanks. He then scattered corn for their chickens.

His chores done, Henri walked toward the house. Like most habitant homes, it was built of logs and was low to the ground. The thatched roof was slanted at a steep angle to let the snow slide off. The Berniers' two windows were covered with oiled paper—only rich people could afford glass. Homes had few windows because they let in cold air in winter and heat in summer. Though the windows faced south to let in as much light as possible, there was little natural light inside.

Indeed, Henri had to squint at first to see in the near darkness of the home's single room. A fireplace on the far wall provided the strongest light. As he entered, Charlotte turned from the fireplace. Her light brown hair was covered with a white

"No." Henri shrugged.

"The taxes pay for leather buckets that hold water to put out the fires!" Papa threw back his head and laughed and so did Henri. Yet worry, like a small worm, wriggled through his mind. Should he fear living in Québec City because of fires? What else was there to fear?

Papa flicked the reins and Mimi turned down the road toward the lower city. Québec was also a shipping port, and as they descended the hill, Henri stared at the St. Lawrence River. It was still frozen but he knew that once the ice melted, it would be filled with ships sailing from France. They would be crammed with goods such as metal tools, pots and pans, and coloured fabrics that the habitants needed and could not make for themselves.

They drove through the city's main square and Henri looked up in awe at a giant cathedral on the hill.

Its stone towers soared into the sky above the massive stone building.

In the country, the habitants' churches were small. This cathedral, Papa said, was almost as grand as the Notre Dame cathedral in Paris.

The lower city was even more crowded than the upper part. The streets were narrow and muddy and filled with garbage. Henri wrinkled his nose at the stench.

Yeech. Papa muttered to himself, "Reminds me of Paris." Back in France, he had lived in Paris for a time, but he quickly grew tired of the crowded city. *It was not for me*, he often told Herni. *Give me the trees and the birds and the open air.* But Henri did have one relative who loved life in the city.

"Pierre Bernier—Carpenter," read a wooden sign over the doorway of a slender stone building. As Henri and his father got out of the sleigh, a tall man with hair and beard the colour of maple syrup and eyes as blue as a robin's egg came out to greet them.

"*Bonjour, bonjour,*" he boomed. "Welcome, Jacques. Welcome, Henri."

Henri smiled. He liked his uncle. Pierre was a good-natured man with a quick smile and large, clever hands.

"You are lucky to be living in Québec," Uncle Pierre said as he led them into his workshop. The floor was carpeted with sawdust and the air smelled of smoke, fresh wood shavings, and candle wax.

"In France, it takes many years to become a craftsman," he said, as he led them to a round wooden table in the corner of the room. "And even then, you are allowed to do only one kind of work. If you make cloth, then that is it." He threw up his hands. "You are allowed only to make cloth. Here we are free to learn and do more than one task. Here, if you make cloth," he smiled, "you can also turn it into clothing."

"And what do you make here as a carpenter that you would not be able to make in France?" asked Henri.

"I fix broken things, and I also make new furniture from the wood of the maple and oak trees that grow around us." His uncle then pointed to a row of wooden dolls on a shelf above the table. "And I also make toys."

Uncle's Pierre's servant, Yvette, appeared with a tray of fresh baked bread, a crock of butter, and a slab of cheese. She set the tray on the table.

Henri nodded to Yvette. She was an older woman, at least forty. Her black hair, streaked with grey, was tucked under her knitted cap. A blue linen apron covered her dark wool skirt. She had worked for Uncle Pierre for many years. Uncle Pierre had never married, which was very unusual. In New France, unmarried men his age were mostly either priests or missionaries. Papa once told Henri the story.

Your uncle Pierre loved a girl from a wealthy family in the upper town. But her family would not hear of the marriage because we Berniers are peasants. Your uncle said that, if he could not marry for love, he would not marry at all. So my stubborn brother has remained a bachelor.

"Would you like some jam with your bread?" Yvette leaned over Henri's shoulder and set a pot of raspberry jam in front of them. She then returned to the fireplace and continued stirring what smelled like a delicious rabbit stew in the big metal pot.

Henri spread a generous helping of jam on his bread and sighed. How good it was to be here. Ever since he was small, he had loved to make things with his hands. Uncle Pierre had taught him to carve, and Henri had made a beautiful wooden cross that hung above the fireplace back at home.

They finished their food and Papa stood. "It is getting late," he said as he looked out the window. "I do not want Charlotte to worry." He patted Henri's shoulder. Then he left the house, climbed into the sleigh, and was gone.

Evening

After Papa left, Henri walked up to his uncle's apartment above the shop. He unpacked his knapsack and placed his things in a small wooden cupboard next to his new bed. Like most townspeople, Uncle Pierre rented his shop and apartment because city property was too expensive to buy. Henri's bed was in a corner of the apartment's main room, while Pierre slept on the other side.

When he was done, Henri went downstairs to the shop. Uncle Pierre had lit candles and the room was illuminated with a soft glow. He was bent over a workbench, sanding a large block of maple wood.

"Henri, come here." He waved him over. "So tell me," he said, setting down the tool, "are you happy to be here?"

Henri sat in a chair facing his uncle. Was he happy to be here? He had always wanted to be a carpenter, to work with his hands and make beautiful furniture from wood.

Yet until today, he had not realized what such a move truly meant.

"You will see that we live a good life in Québec City. We work hard but we enjoy ourselves, too." He clapped Henri on the shoulder. "Now we will eat our supper and then you must sleep. Tomorrow you begin your work as a carpenter."

How could all this happen in one day? thought Henri as he lay in bed. He had awakened on the farm to his usual chores and breakfast with his family. But then, he'd climbed into the sleigh and ridden away from home to a brand-new life. What would Charlotte do without him to bring her wood? Would Antoine be a more obedient son than he? And most of all, would Marie learn not to miss him?

Henri stared into the darkness and suddenly he knew what he wanted to do. He would learn woodworking from Uncle Pierre. He would work hard and make his family proud. And when he went home for the wedding, he would bring everyone presents that he had made with his own two hands. For Charlotte he would make a box of maple wood; for Papa he would carve a pipe and a walking stick. Antoine would get a rod he could use to catch fish, and Marie and Jacqueline, dolls like the ones Uncle Pierre had on the shelf in his workroom.

Yes, that is what he would do, Henri decided as he drifted off to sleep. He would use the skills he would learn in his new life to make beautiful things for the people he loved in his old life at home.

NOUVELLE FRANCE

Henri

Breaking New Ground:
The Habitants

In 1627, the French government was trying to bring settlers to the colony of New France. They gave wealthy French lords, called seigneurs, large tracts of land to supervise. The seigneurs could then give a section of their land to anyone who asked for it. In return for land to farm, peasants gave their seigneur a portion of their crops every year. We peasants were called habitants.

At first habitant houses were built of wood, but later houses were made of stone. During the spring and summer we cleared the land, planted and harvested crops, and tended the livestock. We built large barns to give our animals shelter during the winter, and stored food and firewood to last through the cold months.

Fur traders traveled north to trade European goods such as axes, cooking pots, blankets, and cloth to the Natives for the pelts of beavers, foxes, and other animals. Habitants also adopted some of the Native clothing, wearing moccasins and using animal skins for coats, gloves, and hats.

The inside of my old habitant home was a lot like this.

Habitant families needed to collect firewood to heat their homes.

We learned how to use snowshoes and how to hunt and fish in the local land. During winter, when there was little work on the farms, we enjoyed playing cards, board games, and music. There were village dances and feasts with family and neighbours at the New Year.

Wealthy people attended formal dances at the governor's palace in Québec City. They liked to dress the way rich people dressed in France and favoured clothes of silk, wool, and velvet. Women wore fancy hats trimmed with feathers and other ornaments. All the hats were made by hand, and much of the clothing was imported from France.

As the colony grew, a wealthy merchant class developed in the larger towns of Québec and Montréal (which was founded in 1642). By this time, habitants made most of the things we needed such as clothing and furniture. We imported the things from Europe that we could not make such as pots, salt, and guns.

This is a drawing of Québec City in 1740. By this time, the city had grown from the one I knew as a child.

QUEBEC.

A. The Fort.
B. The Recollets.
C. The Platform.
D. The Jesuits.
E. The Cathedral.
F. The Seminary.
G. The Hôtel Dieu.
H. The Bishop's House.
I. The Redoubt.
K. The Hospital.

The Sugaring Off

Upper Canada, 1795

Sally sat up in bed with a start. She shivered and pulled the quilt up to the tip of her nose. Her sister, Edith, stirred beside her but didn't wake. Sally looked around the room. Dusky light filtered through the pale brown linen curtains at the window. It must be around six o'clock.

What was it that had awakened her? And then she remembered. Today was sugaring-off day—the day she and her family would turn the sap from the maple trees into syrup. She ran her tongue over her lips. She could already taste the sticky sweetness of this special treat.

Closing her eyes, Sally allowed herself to drift back to sleep, but not for long. A few minutes later her mother came into the room and shook her awake. "Get up sleepy head. You too, Edith," she said as Edith turned away from her voice. "We have lots to do and no time to waste. Papa and Tim are already outside feeding the animals."

Sally jumped out of bed. "Edith! Today is the sugaring off!"

"It's cold." Edith slid lower under the covers.

"Up, up, up." Sally mimicked her mother's voice. She pulled the quilt down to the foot of the bed.

"Stop that," Edith screamed. "Just once in my life I would like to sleep until the sun is all the way up in the sky," she sighed as she got out of bed.

"You did that last winter, when you had influenza. In fact, you slept for three days."

"That does not count," Edith sniffed. "I wish Mama and Papa had stayed in Scotland, where life is civilized."

Sally ignored her. She was used to her sister's grumbling—she was just like their mother.

Mama had come to Upper Canada as a young wife, unready for the harsh realities of life on a backwoods pioneer homestead. Her family had lived in a comfortable house in a village outside of Edinburgh. Her father was a baker with a shop on the main street. On her marriage, Mama had expected to live a similar life.

But Papa wanted his own farm. This was a dream he could not realize in Scotland. Then a friend who had settled in Upper Canada sent him a letter saying that good fertile land could be bought cheap there. Papa decided that this was his only chance, so he brought his wife and young daughter across the ocean to a new land.

How often had Sally heard the story of their difficult crossing? Her parents and Edith were crammed into the hold of a sailing ship along with dozens of other passengers. The family shared one bunk. The voyage took six weeks, during which time they were often sick from rough weather. The ship's hold stank from the slop pails used as toilets, bad food, and unwashed bodies all crammed into a small, airless space.

Edith tied an apron over her heavy blue wool dress and then peered into the small mirror nailed to the bedroom wall.

"If we still lived in Scotland, I would have pretty clothes. I wouldn't have to wear such a dull, scratchy wool dress."

"Papa says it's cold in Scotland, too," Sally said, pulling on her own clothing.

Edith was fifteen. She was the only one of the Benson children born in Scotland—a fact that she loved to bring up often. *As if she remembered it*, Sally thought as she slipped a coarse linen apron over her head. Edith was only two years old when Mama and Papa came to Canada. Sally was born the next year, and Tim three years later. To hear Edith talk, however, you would think she had been raised in Edinburgh Castle.

Sally shivered. March was a cold, damp month, but she didn't mind. She knew that spring would soon follow. She could hardly wait for the snow to melt so she could scour the forest for wild greens such as leeks and cow cabbage. It had been a long time since they had eaten fresh vegetables. By March all that was left in the root cellar were potatoes, a few carrots, and parsnips. Mama added these to the soups and stews she made with the occasional squirrel or rabbit that Papa caught. Otherwise, their winter diet consisted mostly of porridge, dried peas, and the salted pork from the barrel.

The sugaring off was the last winter ritual before the snow melted. Once the ground thawed, Papa would plant corn, oats, potatoes, and wheat, and Mama would start her kitchen garden. *And the hens will lay eggs again*, Sally thought. *It would be nice to have fresh eggs right now.*

Sally finished brushing her long brown hair and tied it back with a piece of string. She bent down and tightened the laces on her boots. Edith was still primping in front of the mirror, so Sally walked into the main room of their cabin.

When Papa bought the land, the first thing he did was build a shanty where the family lived for a year. The following spring, with the help of neighbours, he constructed the log house. First they cleared the ground of rocks, which they used to build the house's foundation. Next they chopped down trees—over one hundred of them—for the logs that made up the walls and the fences. The house had one main room, two bedrooms—one for Mama and Papa and another for the girls—and a loft where Tim slept. The shanty was now home to their cow and two pigs.

As Sally entered the front room, Mama turned from the stone fireplace. She had just finished ladling bowls of porridge from the black kettle hanging from a hook over the fire.

"Here, Sally, set these on the table. Papa and your brother will be starving when they come in." She slapped at a spark on her dress. Cooking at a fireplace was dangerous. Sparks and soot were constantly flying through the air, and more than once, Mama's dress had caught fire. Now she was extra careful and warned everyone to be that way, too.

Sally took the bowls. She would rather be doing chores with Papa and Tim than setting the table every morning. So what if Tim was a boy? She was as strong as him. Well, never mind. She'd show Papa how strong she was at the sugaring off. Lugging those heavy buckets of sap was hard work.

She set the bowls on the table. Next she took tin mugs for tea down from the shelf and put them beside the bowls. Tomorrow she would be able to put out a jug of fresh maple syrup. She smacked her lips in anticipation.

"It is very cold out there." Papa came into the room rubbing his hands. They were red and chapped. Tim was right behind him.

"Here, Sally, catch." Tim tossed her an icicle. "You can cover it in syrup later."

"It will melt, silly." Sally popped the tip of the icicle in her mouth. "I'll just eat it now."

Mama was getting impatient. "Everyone sit down. The porridge is getting cold."

"Are you ready for the sugaring off?" Papa smiled at them down the length of the table. "The sap is running strong this year. We will get a good batch of syrup."

Tim grinned. "Mama, will you make pancakes tomorrow so we can drown them in syrup?"

"Yes," smiled Edith. "I love pancakes with maple syrup."

"You'll have to wait for pancakes until the chickens start laying their eggs," said Mama. "But porridge is also good with maple syrup."

"You would not have maple syrup in Scotland," Sally said to her sister with a sly smile. "Hurry up. Let's wash the dishes. We don't want Papa to start without us."

Afternoon

Edith might like *eating* the maple syrup, but she certainly wasn't happy about the *making* of it. Sally watched her sister lift the bucket of sap from the wooden spigot that had been inserted into the sapwood, the outer layer of the tree. Sap flowed through the spigot and into the pail.

"It's heavy," Edith said as she handed it to Sally.

"I can handle it." Sally clutched the bucket with both hands. It *was* heavy. She set it in the snow and pulled her mittens up so they fit tight across her hands. Next she adjusted her wool shawl so it covered her ears and draped across her shoulders. Bending down, the way Papa had shown her, she grasped the bucket with both hands and cradled it against her chest. It was filled with what looked like water. Only when boiled down would it develop the dark, sticky sweetness of maple syrup.

Sally followed the path through the trees to the clearing. Her boots sank into the soft snow. The hem of her dress, wet from the snow, clung to her ankles, making it difficult to walk. She paused and set the bucket down. She looked up at the sky. It was clear and very blue. In another month the geese would return. Sally could picture them in their V-formation soaring overhead—happy to be home.

As she arrived at the clearing Tim came up. "You're pretty strong for a girl."

"Thanks, Tim." Sally handed the bucket to him. She often felt closer to her brother than she did to Edith. As small children, she and Tim had been playmates during long, cold winters. They both loved the outdoors. Tim had taught her to climb the big maple tree in front of the house. He had taught her to dig for worms and put them on a hook and use them to catch fish in the river.

Tim carried the bucket to the middle of the clearing, where Papa had built a roaring fire. Three kettles hung over the flames. Sally watched Papa and her brother pour the sap into the first kettle until it was filled almost to the top. As the sap heated up and boiled, the water in it evaporated, and the sap thickened. She looked into the second kettle, where an earlier batch of boiled sap was being further reduced to sweet, sticky syrup. Later on, some of that syrup would go into the third kettle, where it would be boiled over a smaller fire until it turned into dark brown sugar. The sugar would then be packed into wooden boxes and stored for use in the winter.

"Here." Tim handed her the paddle with which he had been stirring the mixture in the second kettle. "You stir for a while."

Sally wrapped her hands around the paddle. Pushing it through the thickening mixture was hard work. The wood from the paddle rubbed her skin, right through the wool of her mittens. Hot steam clouded her eyes.

The first year she had been allowed to help, a drop of syrup as hot as a cinder splashed on her cheek. She still had the scar. Now she was very careful.

"How is the syrup coming?" Mama peered into the kettle. "It looks good."

"It's beautiful." Sally loved watching as the syrup turned from clear to light brown and finally to a rich golden colour. She wished her boring brown hair could be the colour of maple syrup.

"I'm going back to the house to start making supper." Mama patted Sally's shoulder. "Now you be careful. I don't want any accidents." Sally watched her mother make her way back to the house. Her father had gone to get more wood for the fire and she was alone. She kept stirring the syrup. It was getting thicker and her arms were tired. Where were Tim and Edith? They should each take a turn.

Suddenly Edith raced into the clearing. Her hair, so carefully plaited this morning, was flying every which way, and her dress was streaked with mud.

Sally stared at her. She had never seen her sister so agitated.

"What is wrong, Edith? What happened?"

Edith looked like she was going to cry. "Tim," she said. "Tim..."

"What is wrong with Tim?"

Edith stood as if turned to stone; her eyes were wide with fear.

Sally dropped the paddle and shook her. "Edith! What happened to Tim?" Edith snapped out of her trance.

"The river. Ice. He fell through."

Sally's blood turned cold. Softening ice was a serious danger in spring. Tim knew that. What was he doing on the river? She started to run, with Edith on her heels. *What should she do?* She called out for Mama and Papa. No one answered.

"Let's go," she said to Edith.

Crashing through the underbrush, the girls reached the riverbank. Tim was about five feet from shore, his upper body sticking up through a hole in the ice. He was clutching the edge of the ice. Sally looked around for something for him to hold on to.

"Here." Edith picked up a broken tree branch.

Sally took it and lay down on her stomach, grasping the branch and stretching it out toward Tim. He reached for it but the branch was a few inches too short. Even from this distance, Sally could tell that his lips were turning blue.

If she didn't get him out soon, he would freeze or, worse, lose his grip and slip under the ice.

"Hold on to my feet!" she shouted to Edith.

"What are you going to do?"

"I'm going to slide out toward him."

"You'll fall in, too!"

"The ice over here is solid." Sally pointed to her right. "If I move my upper body onto it, Tim can grab the branch. Just hold my feet and hang on to them."

Edith dropped to her knees and clutched Sally's ankles as Sally carefully inched onto the ice. Stretching her arm as far as it would go, she pointed the branch at Tim. This time he grabbed it.

"Edith, help me pull!"

Sally and Edith tugged on the branch. Slowly, painfully, Tim inched toward them until he was able to hoist himself out of the water. A moment later, they were all standing on the riverbank, wet, trembling, and hugging each other.

When they got back to the fire, they found their father calling out for them.

"Where have you been?" Papa exploded. Then his voice softened. "Let's get back to the house so you can get out of those wet clothes before you all catch pneumonia."

Later, when warmed up, Tim told the story. "Sally and Edith saved me," he said.

"Tim, what were you doing on the river?" Sally asked, when they had all warmed their hands over the fire.

"I was going to surprise everyone and catch a fish. I thought we could roast it for dinner and have it with the maple syrup."

At the mention of the syrup, Sally stared at the kettle. "Is it ruined? Did it burn?"

"No." Her father sighed. "You and Edith saved Tim. I only saved the syrup."

Evening

After they had changed into clean, dry clothes and consumed what seemed like gallons of hot tea, the children gathered at the table for dinner. Mama had lit a fat tallow candle, and the flame filled the room with a soft glow and a warm smell.

"I'm sorry about the fish," Tim stammered.

Papa shook his head. "What you did was very dangerous, Tim."

"I was ice fishing, like you taught me," said Tim. He looked about ready to cry.

His father placed an arm around his shoulder. "That was very thoughtful, Tim, but you should never ice fish alone, especially in spring. The ice is starting to melt."

"But I wanted to bring home a special dinner."

"I have something much better than fish," Mama said excitedly. "A surprise." She set a huge platter of pancakes and a jug of maple syrup in front of them.

Sally's eyes widened. "How did you make pancakes without eggs?"

"Our chickens know it's spring, too. I found two fresh eggs this morning."

After dinner, Mama prepared dough for the morning's bread. Tonight she was making potato bread. She mixed leftover mashed potatoes with flour and salt, then added yeast and water. The dough would rise overnight. In the morning she would punch it down, let it rise again, and then bake it in a iron pan covered with coals.

Tim went up to his loft, and Sally and Edith to their bedroom. Shivering in the chill night air, the girls quickly got into their nightclothes, slipped into bed, and pulled the quilt right up to their noses.

"Edith, how did you know that Tim was at the river?" Sally asked.

"I was coming to help you with the syrup and I heard a cry."

"I'm very glad you were there."

"I am too." Both girls were quiet for a moment, softly breathing as their bodies grew warmer beneath the quilt. "Sally, I don't really want to live in Scotland."

"I know," Sally said. "Life here is hard sometimes, but it can be good too. Like today, with the maple syrup."

She waited for Edith's reply, but her sister was already fast asleep.

sally

My Life as a Settler:
The Pioneers

Most of the pioneers who settled in Upper Canada, like my family, came from European countries such as England, Scotland, Italy, and Germany. Land was expensive in these countries and moving to Canada was our only chance to own property. My parents had to endure a long and dangerous sea voyage to get to Canada. Many people on board their ship suffered from malnutrition or a disease called scurvy, caused by a lack of vitamin C.

Thankfully, the local Natives taught us many things, like how to brew the barks of spruce and juniper trees to make a tea full of vitamin C. We learned to sew clothing out of animal skins, and to preserve meat by drying it over a fire or in the sun. Best of all, they taught us my favourite thing—how to tap into maple trees and make maple syrup!

Building a homestead was a lot of hard work.

Before we could farm our new land, we first had to clear it by cutting down trees and removing the stumps. We used this wood to build our houses, and to make furniture and farm equipment such as wooden yokes for oxen. For the first planting we used seeds we had brought from our home countries. We planted things like rye, wheat, and oats, along with fruits and vegetables. After the harvest, we saved seeds from the best plants and used them the following year.

We pioneers made most of the things we used, and everyone worked, including children. The women provided food and clothing for the family. The husband was the farmer who cleared land, built farm buildings, and tended to the livestock. Girls like myself learned domestic chores such as cooking, sewing, making cheese and butter, and tending the kitchen garden. The boys worked with their fathers in the fields.

Animals were an important part of a farm. We raised chickens and geese, kept sheep for wool, and had oxen and horses to pull our plows and wagons. Pigs were common because they were easy to care for and not very fussy about what they ate.

Collecting sap was the first step in making maple syrup.

Slowly, small towns grew across Upper Canada. Our lives became a little easier.

As more and more settlers came to Upper Canada, towns and villages slowly developed. This allowed families like ours to trade or sell our extra products, such as vegetables or butter, for other things we needed, such as wool or sugar. Later on, businesses developed to provide services and supplies for the farmers. There was even a market where we could sell our crops. Once these changes came, life on our farm became a little easier and we didn't have to work quite so hard.

A Big Decision

Buxton, Ontario, 1863

Morning

Amos opened one eye, saw that it was still dark, and pulled the covers over his head. He wriggled closer to Isaac, his fourteen-year-old brother, who was taking up most of the bed. In the last year, Isaac had grown so tall that Amos thought he should have his own bed. But Mamma said they had to share, and wasn't this a whole lot better than sleeping on the floor like they used to in the slave cabin? Of course it was, but at twelve, Amos was getting bigger too. He scrunched his eyes closed. Maybe he could sleep a few more minutes.

"Time to get up," Mamma called out as she entered the room.

"It's the middle of the night," Isaac grumbled. He flopped over and his arm landed smack on Amos's face.

"Hey, get off me." Amos shoved him aside, and Isaac sprang into a sitting position.

"Don't you go hittin' me," he said, balling his fists.

"You keep pushin' me off the bed and I'll hit you good."

"Now stop fightin', you two." Mamma's skirt swished across the floor as she walked to the window and pulled back the curtain. A rush of cool air raised goosebumps over Amos's skin. "You have to do the chores before church. The Reverend Douglas's gonna speak about the war to end slavery in the United States."

Isaac sat up and rubbed his eyes. "I'm going down there and fight."

"Hush. I don't want to hear any talk of you going off to fight in other people's war. Now get up, both of you."

"It's our war, too," Isaac protested.

"We fought our war by escapin' from Master Wrigley and coming to Canada."

Isaac yawned. "I know that, Mamma. I want to help the rest of our people get free."

"Maybe first you should get dressed so you can help your father with the chores," she said, eyeing Isaac before turning to Amos. "And you too."

After Amos had washed up at the water pump he crossed the yard to the hen house. A chorus of cackles greeted him as he gathered six eggs and placed them in his basket. "Hush, you dumb chickens," he scolded. "You're lucky I'm not takin' you in the kitchen so Mamma can make you into soup."

As he walked back toward the house, Amos marvelled at the joy of being free. His family had arrived in Canada and the Buxton Settlement five years earlier, after a dangerous month-long journey on the Underground Railroad.

Of course, it wasn't *really* a railroad: it was a route slaves took when they escaped to freedom in the North. Many good people had hidden them, given them food and a place to sleep. Once, when Amos had a high fever, a Quaker woman had even helped nurse him back to health. There were times, however, when his family had been on their own, hiding in the woods by day, walking at night, and going hungry when they ran out of food. Today they had not only their own house—which he had helped his father and brother build—but two cows, six pigs, a horse named Betsy, a coop full of chickens, and fifty acres of land where they grew wheat, corn, and vegetables.

Amos crossed the front stoop of the house and walked into the parlour. Mamma was setting a bowl of porridge in the middle of the long wooden table.

"Here're the eggs." Amos gave her the basket. Then he walked to the fireplace and warmed his hands over the fire. Amos was proud of the fireplace. It was red brick from the settlement's own brickyard. It had a wide mantel where Mamma kept candles, pots of dried flowers, and a green glass pitcher she had bought off a peddler man who came through the settlement last summer.

As he turned to the table, Amos heard boots stomping and the door swung open. Pa and Isaac came in, rubbing the early morning chill from their hands.

"Where's that hot breakfast you promised me, Martha?" Pa boomed.

"Hush. It's right in front of your face." Mamma laughed as chairs scraped back and the men settled down.

Mamma took her place and bowed her head while Pa said grace. Amos hoped his stomach would stop growling long enough for him to say "Amen." The minute Pa was through, he handed Mamma his bowl and she ladled porridge into it. Amos poured thick cream over it and dug in.

"I hear a new family arrived last night," said Pa around mouthfuls of porridge. "A ma, pa, and two young 'uns: a boy named Tom—about your age, Amos—and Ruth, a ten-year-old girl."

"Where're they staying?" asked Mamma.

"With the pastor and his wife." Pa sighed. "They're real sad. They had two more children, but their master sold 'em before they could escape."

"Oh my." Mamma's eyes got shiny with tears. "It's good they got here before he sold the other two. They're gonna need stuff to get 'em started."

Amos could already see his mamma bustling through the storage shed at the back of the house, pulling out extra bedding, clothes she'd saved from the boys, and pots and pans she could spare. *You gotta always be ready to help one another,* she would often tell him.

Pa stood and pushed back his chair. "Finish your breakfast, boys, and change outta them work clothes. We gonna be late for church."

Afternoon

"That Reverend Douglas sure can preach." Pa shook his head.

"He's got a golden tongue, all right," said Mamma slowly. They were back at the table eating her excellent Sunday dinner of roast chicken, carrots, and mashed potatoes. "I know he's a good man but I don't like him telling our men folk to go and fight in that war in the United States."

"Like the reverend said, it's *our* war too, Ma." Isaac waved a drumstick in the air. "Them's our people being kept as slaves."

"And there's a whole army fightin' to free 'em," she countered quickly, looking at Isaac. "We have work to do here, farmin' our land and making a home for those who escape slavery and join us." She turned to her husband. "I heard the men talkin' 'bout a house raisin' next week."

"We're gonna build a place for that new family. They'll get fifty acres, like the rest of us, and we'll help 'em get started with a house and clearin' the land."

He turned to Isaac. "That's how you can help. You too, Amos. We have to dig a drainage ditch around their property, like we did on ours. It keeps the water from puddlin' up on the land, so the crops can grow proper."

Amos grinned. "I like choppin' down trees, Pa."

"Clearin' land ain't gonna free the slaves." Isaac jumped up, knocking over his chair. "Fightin's gonna free 'em, and that's what I'm gonna do."

"Isaac, are you really gonna run off and join the Union Army?" Amos pushed aside the book he was reading and studied his brother, who was staring out the front window.

"Reverend Douglas said it's our duty. You heard him in church this morning," replied Isaac. He turned around and looked right at Amos.

"We're free, Amos, and we gotta help the rest of our people be free too."

Amos shook his head. "He was talkin' to grown men. We're not grown yet."

"I am!" Isaac poked a finger at his chest. "I'm fourteen, and if Ma and Pa don't let me go, I'm gonna run away."

"You'll do nothin' of the sort." Their mother came in holding a fresh-baked pie in one hand and a Bible in the other. She set the pie on the window sill to cool.

"That sure smells good, Mamma," said Amos, licking his lips.

"It's the last of the apples." She looked out the window at the bare trees and sighed. "This time of year, I get a yearning for green leaves and fresh fruit."

"It's almost April, and we'll soon be seeing buds on the trees."

"So we will, Amos." Mamma smiled. She stroked his hair. "How about, while that pie's coolin', you give me another readin' lesson?"

"Yes, ma'am," Amos beamed. Like all slaves, his parents had never learned to read or write. It was against the law for them to even try.

As they sat, Isaac moved to the door. "I'm goin' outside."

"Come sit with us and practice your readin' too."

Isaac ignored her and left.

Mamma frowned. "I don't know what I'm gonna do with that boy."

"He'll be all right." Amos opened the family Bible. "Mamma, let's read the story about Jonah. I like the part where the whale swallows him all up."

Evening

"Hey, Betsy, how're you doing tonight?" Amos walked over to the stall where the family's horse was standing. He picked up a stiff bristled brush and started grooming her flanks. She whinnied and shook her head. "You like that, don't you? *Whew.*" He pinched his nose. "You sure have been busy today. I'll clean it up."

Betsy lifted her head and gazed at him out of big brown eyes. Amos reached in his pocket and pulled out a sugar cube. "Don't tell Mamma I gave you this. Promise?" The horse licked his hand. "That tickles," Amos laughed. He finished tidying up her stall, then left the barn and picked up the slop pail to feed the pigs.

He looked over to the house. Mamma and Pa were sitting in their rockers on the front stoop. Mamma was sewing. She never threw anything away. Every bit of material went into her scrap basket and came back as curtains or a shirt for him or Isaac. Tonight she was working on the quilt she would enter at the summer quilting bee. Mamma said this one showed the route, based on the North Star, that slaves followed when they escaped to freedom.

Pa was sleeping in his chair with a newspaper across his lap. Amos knew it was *The Provincial Freeman*, published by one of their neighbours, Mary Ann Shadd. Pa still couldn't read too well, so sometimes Amos read parts of the paper to him. His pa liked that paper because Ms. Shadd said that former slaves should think of Canada as their forever home. He spent hours arguing with grumpy Mr. Pike, who lived on the next farm. Old Man Pike said that when the United States freed the slaves, they should all go back. There had been some real screaming matches over that one.

The hoot of an owl reminded Amos that it was getting late. He picked up the bucket and was crossing the yard when a shrill whistle stopped him in his tracks. Charcoal shadows stretched across the ground and everything felt still and hidden in their yard. Amos felt the hair on the back of his neck jump, like the hackles on Betsy's back when an animal skittered across her path.

"Pssst, Amos." Isaac emerged from the tall grass on the far side of the barn with a finger to his lips.

Amos set down the pail so hard the slops splashed onto his pants.

"Isaac!" he hissed. "What you doin' scarin' me like that?"

"Didn't know you was such a scaredy cat."

"Why're you whisperin'?"

"Don't want Mamma and Pa to hear me."

"Why not?"

"'Cause they'd try to stop me."

"Stop you from what?" Amos's eyes widened. "You're not runnin' off to join that army, are you?"

Isaac slowly bobbed his head up and down. "I gotta help free our people."

"You might get killed."

"Take care of Mamma and Pa while I'm gone, you hear?"

Amos started to protest, but Isaac grabbed his shoulder. "That's an order." He turned and disappeared into the shadows.

Amos watched him go, too stunned to react. *What should he do?* If he told on Isaac, he'd be a snitch and Isaac would hate him for life. If he didn't, Isaac might get killed, and Mamma and Pa would hate him for life.

Amos stared in the direction Isaac had gone. Soon his brother would be impossible to find in the darkening woods. In a flash, Amos made up his mind.

"Mamma, Pa," he shouted running toward the stoop. "Get up, get up."

His mother dropped her sewing as both his parents ran toward him.

His father reached him first. "Amos, what is it? What's wrong?"

"Is it slave catchers?" his mother asked. She was breathing hard and her eyes were round as marbles.

"It's Isaac."

"Isaac?" Pa looked around, his eyes squinting into the dusk. "Where is he?"

"He gone."

"Gone?" Mamma's hand flew to her heart. "Where?" she whispered.

"He goin' to join the Union Army."

Pa's face got a look on it angrier than Amos had ever seen. His arms, strong and muscled from years of working the land, came up into fists, as if he were ready for a fight. "Martha," he said, "you and Amos go into the house. I'm going to find Isaac and bring him back."

"I wanna go with you."

"Amos…" His father gave him that "I mean business look" that meant he'd better do what he said.

Amos followed his mother into the house. They went into the parlour. Mamma lit some candles and walked to the fireplace. She stirred the embers until tongues of flame licked the edges of the logs. "What has gotten into that boy?" She sighed, turning to look at Amos.

"He hates slavery," said Amos. "I do too," he added.

"We all hate slavery." His mother touched her eyes with her apron. "That doesn't mean a child can go fight in a war he knows nothin' about."

"Isaac thinks he knows all about it." Amos sat at the table and propped his chin in his hands. Mamma sat across from him. Neither of them spoke for what seemed like hours. Amos must have dozed off because when his eyes opened, he saw Pa and Isaac standing across the room, both of them dripping wet.

"You coulda caught your death," Mamma said as she opened the cupboard and pulled out two wool blankets.

"I caught up with Isaac at the river. He was about to steal a canoe. We scuffled and then—"

"Fell in," Mamma finished for him. "And you. What're you doing stealin'—"

"I was gonna leave it on the other side," Isaac said. He glared at Amos. "Why'd you tell 'em I was goin'?" He grabbed the blanket and stomped off to his room.

Later, in bed, Amos thought about what had happened. He felt guilty about telling on Isaac, yet at the same time, he believed he had done the right thing. *How could I be right and wrong at the same time?* wondered Amos. He turned on his side and stared at Isaac lying on his back, arms folded under his head.

"You mad at me?"

"What do you think?"

"You gonna run away again?"

"Don't know."

Amos thought for a minute. "Pa says we're doin' an important job right here by showin' that black people can live as good as anybody, once we get the chance."

"Black people gotta be free to get here first."

"*We* got here, Isaac." Amos sat up and looked down at his brother. "I was thinkin' about that new kid in church. He looked as scared as we were when we first came. You an' me, we can teach him to read and help Pa and the other men build his family a house. That's a way of freein' slaves too."

Isaac didn't answer. Amos turned over and buried his face in the pillow. His brother, he decided, would have to figure things out for himself. But he knew what he was going to do. Tomorrow he'd make friends with that new boy and his sister and help them learn all the good things there were to know about being free.

Buxton

Amos

Our Journey to Freedom:
The Underground Railroad

Against their will, black people first came to North America as slaves. They were captured in Africa and shipped across the ocean. My parents were born in the southern United States. Like most slaves, they worked on a large cotton farm called a plantation. Slaves had no freedom or rights. It was even against the law for anyone to teach a slave to read or write—plantation owners were afraid literate slaves might learn how to escape.

In 1793, Lieutenant-Governor Simcoe abolished slavery in Upper Canada (now Ontario). By the early 1800s, there were a lot of Americans who wanted to do the same. They were called abolitionists. But in 1850, the United States Congress passed the Fugitive Slave Law. It allowed bounty hunters to capture blacks and sell them into slavery in the South, even if they had been born free in the North.

My family escaped from a cotton plantation like this in the southern United States.

Many of my people risked their lives to reach Canada on the Underground Railroad.

Canada became the safest place for blacks to live. A network of people opposed to slavery formed the Underground Railroad. It helped slaves escape to the northern United States and Canada. It was called "underground" because it had to be kept secret.

Most of the blacks who came to Canada settled in areas around either St. Catharines or Windsor, Ontario. With the help of others, some started their own towns. One of these was the Elgin Settlement, also known as Buxton. That's where we went once we were in Canada.

Buxton was started by the Reverend William King. He believed that blacks would succeed if they had all of the same opportunities as whites. He felt that for the settlement to be stable, the people who lived there should pay for their own land, live on it, and work it for at least ten years. He established a school for black and white children. By the mid 1860s, there were 2,000 people living in Buxton.

In 1861 the Civil War broke out in the United States. The North, which wanted to abolish slavery, was called the Union. The South was the Confederacy. Seventy men from Buxton returned to the United States to fight with the Union Army. When the war ended in 1865, the slaves were finally freed. Many of the black people in Canada returned to the United States to look for their families. Those who stayed in Buxton helped the settlement survive as a small farming community.

This is Main Street in South Buxton.

Bridget's Concert

The Annex, Toronto, 1900

Morning

Dear Annie,

Since you and I will be talking every day, I thought you should have a better name than "Diary." So I've named you "Annie" after my favourite aunt. She gave you to me yesterday for my twelfth birthday. You are so beautiful, with your red leather binding and gold clasp. I've put your key on a red velvet ribbon and I wear it around my neck.

Today is a special day, at least for my mother. We are going to the Worthingtons' for tea. That means I have to dress up in that linen dress with the leg o' mutton sleeves that makes me feel like a Sunday roast. Mrs. Worthington is a distant cousin of the Queen's great-great-grandmother, so by Toronto standards, her whole family is royal. But the way Mother carries on about them, you would think we were being introduced to Queen Victoria herself. What a lot of hogwash! Don't you agree?

Sometimes I wish we were still living in our old house in the city. Father does too, although he won't admit it. He gets impatient with what he calls Mother's "fancy airs." "Just because we are lucky and have made some money does not mean we have to change," he had said when Mother insisted we move to the Annex. Maybe I should explain about the Annex.

It is the area north of the city where the rich are building homes. Timothy Eaton, *who owns T. Eaton Company, has a huge mansion up the hill at 182 Lowther Street. Then the Gooderhams, who own the Gooderham and Worts Distillery, built their mansion at the corner of Bloor and St. George Streets. Since Father's store is across the street from Mr. Eaton's, Mother insisted we live near him too.*

Father felt that wasn't right. The way that he saw it, "We may be rich but we are Irish, not British. We are not royal."

To which Mother answered, "Nonsense. This is 1900, not the Middle Ages."

So Father gave in and we are living in a luxurious house on Lowther Avenue, near Spadina. We have indoor plumbing with flush toilets and electric lights and a telephone in the kitchen. Which is all good, but now Mother wants to "launch" me into Toronto society. At least she isn't sending me to finishing school. Rich girls, like Elizabeth Worthington, are tutored at home until they are thirteen and then sent to finishing school to prepare them for their "coming out" at fifteen. Father did put his foot down about that, so I'll just be home tutored instead.

"Miss Bridget." Clara, the O'Sheas' maid, knocked on the door. "Your mother wants you downstairs in the breakfast room."

"Rats. I'm coming," Bridget called out. *I'm sorry, Annie. I'll have to get back to you later,* she wrote and set the diary on her dresser. With a quick glance in the mirror to make sure her hair was still in the sleek red braid that Clara had plaited for her, she left the room.

Clara looked Bridget up and down and then sighed. "Not perfect, but you will have to do. Now go down before your mother has your hide, and mine as well."

Bridget raced down the stairs, lifting her skirt so she wouldn't trip. She barely resisted the urge to slide down the banister. When she reached the bottom she stopped, took a deep breath, and entered the breakfast room. Her mother was sitting at the end of the table pouring coffee from a silver pot. As usual, Mrs. O'Shea was immaculately groomed. Her hair, the same coppery red as Bridget's, was piled on top of her head. She wore a stiff white blouse with a high lace collar and an ivory cameo brooch at her throat.

"Good morning, Mother." Bridget executed a slight curtsy. She had learned how to do this by watching Elizabeth Worthington greet her parents. Bridget thought it was silly but it pleased her mother.

Mrs. O'Shea nodded. "You are late. As usual," she added under her breath.

"Leave the girl alone." Mr. O'Shea put down his *Globe* newspaper and smiled at Bridget. "Good morning, kitten."

Bridget smiled back at her father. She thought he looked especially handsome in his black suit and starched white shirt, with his neatly trimmed beard and mustache.

Bridget slid into a chair beside her brother, Robbie, who was nine. Robbie ignored her and concentrated on his bowl of porridge, sketching the shape of a horse in the maple syrup topping.

Mrs. O'Shea rang the silver bell beside her plate. Margaret, the kitchen maid, scurried in and placed a bowl of steaming porridge in front of Bridget. *Porridge again?* She would have preferred a boiled egg and sausage, but one tradition Mother had brought with them to the Annex was good Irish porridge for breakfast. Bridget reached for the cream and slathered it over her cereal. In spite of her distaste, she was hungry and ate quickly.

"Slow down, Bridget," her mother instructed. "If you want to be treated like a lady, you must act like a lady."

Bridget set her spoon into the bowl. The spoon was silver, the bowl a thin white China. Too dainty, her father often complained, adding that he preferred the thick crockery they had used at their home in the city.

Mr. O'Shea folded his paper and set it neatly beside his coffee cup. "And so, kitten, what are you up to today?"

Mrs. O'Shea answered quickly for her daughter: "Mr. Carrington will be here at nine for her diction lesson and Miss Brown, her piano teacher, at eleven. And this afternoon," she continued, lifting her chin, "we are invited to Eudora Worthington's home for tea."

"Ugh!" Bridget wrinkled her nose.

"Bridget, you should be flattered that Mrs. Worthington has asked us."

"You can visit with Elizabeth." Robbie flashed an impish grin.

Bridget glared at him. She would rather clean chamber pots than spend an afternoon with snobby Elizabeth.

But the Worthingtons' royal connection made them one of the "best" families in Toronto—a fact never lost on Mother.

"Can't I go to the store with you?" Bridget looked wistfully at her father.

"You can come on Saturday," he smiled, and then turned to Robbie. "And what will you do this fine August day?"

"Dennis and I are going to catch frogs in the pond."

"This time don't hide them in your mother's dresser!" Mr. O'Shea stood and tousled Robbie's hair. "I must go. Andrew is waiting outside with the carriage."

Bridget watched her father walk into the front hall, take his hat from the hatstand, and cram it on his head. Before their move to the Annex, he had walked to his store on Yonge Street, whatever the weather. But now they lived too far to walk. A horse-drawn carriage and a driver took him there every morning.

Afternoon

Hi Annie,

At last, I'm alone in my room. You cannot imagine what a rotten afternoon I've had! The Worthingtons' house is like a museum. The maid took us to their parlour, where Mrs. Worthington was sitting in this high-backed chair with carved wooden arms and legs—like a throne. The walls are covered with dark paintings of gloomy people in formal clothes. Mother sat in a chair next to Mrs. Worthington, and Elizabeth and I sat on the sofa facing them.

I guess I should describe Mrs. Worthington. She has blond hair that she wears in two braids on top of her head—like a crown. Her dress was black, even though it is the middle of summer. And she wore a big diamond brooch at her throat and diamonds in her ears. Elizabeth is a younger version of her mother, only she was wearing a light blue dress and her hair is in long curls that bounce on her shoulders every time she nods her head, which she does a lot.

Elizabeth is working hard to be as snobby as her mother. She looked at my dress and asked if it was the latest fashion in Ireland. I told her I've never been to Ireland.

"Oh. But your family is Irish," she said. "My mother says the Irish are different from the rest of us."

And I said, "If we are, it's because we are smarter."

"Well," said Elizabeth, "at least I did not go to public school."

Personally, I preferred the public school, but my mother insists that I have a proper coming-out since Father is a successful tradesman. I think the whole thing is a lot of rubbish. If I had my way, I would continue in public school and work with my father in his store.

Mrs. Worthington then asked me if I like Miss Brown, my piano teacher, because she is looking for someone to teach her five-year-old daughter, Caroline. Now that is a subject I like. In fact, my piano lessons are the highlight of my day. Miss Brown is soft-spoken and in her twenties. She loves music and teaches her pupils to love it, too.

But I should have stayed quiet because after I said all that, Mrs. Worthington asked me to play a piece. And of course, seeing how uncomfortable I was, Elizabeth piped up that she thought it was a great idea. Then my mother gave me that look— the one that means I'd better cooperate or else.

So I was stuck.

I sat down at their grand piano. I have to admit it was wonderful to play such a gorgeous instrument. Our piano is an upright. Anyway, I ran my fingers over the keys and began playing one of the Chopin preludes I've been practising with Miss Brown. Everyone was quiet. I closed my eyes and let the notes ripple across the room. Part of me could have played there all afternoon.

All that changed when I opened my eyes again. One look at Elizabeth and her mother, and suddenly all I wanted was to wipe those smug expressions off their faces. Without even realizing what I was doing, I began to play a popular Irish song, singing at the top of my lungs:

> As I was going over the far-famed Kerry Mountains
> I met with Captain Farrell and his money he was counting
> I first produced me pistol, and then produced me rapier
> Said, "Stand and deliver, for I am a bold deceiver."
>
> Musha ring dumma do damma da
> Whack for the daddy 'o
> Whack for the daddy 'o
> There's whiskey in the jar!

I sang out the last line with gusto, and even repeated the refrain:

> Musha ring dumma do damma da
> Whack for the daddy 'o
> Whack for the daddy 'o
> There's whiskey in the jar!

Needless to say, after that we left in a hurry. So here I am, dear Annie, back in my room, hanging my head in disgrace. Only I don't feel disgraced at all. I feel good. Just don't tell my mother I said that!

Evening

"I have never been so humiliated in my life." Mrs. O'Shea looked down at Bridget, who was slumped in a chair in the family's parlour. "For *our* daughter to insult *Mrs. Worthington* in such a manner! How *could* you embarrass me so?"

"I only did what she asked me to do, Mother." Bridget looked up from under her lashes. "I played the piano."

"There, there, Constance," Mr. O'Shea soothed his wife. "I am sure that your reputation is not forever ruined."

"How would you know? If it were up to you, we would still be mingling with the riffraff in town."

"They weren't such a bad lot. We have good friends in the city."

Bridget left her parents discussing her behaviour and went up to her room. Clara had turned on the light and opened the windows. A soft breeze lifted the white lace curtains. Bridget changed into her nightgown and undid her braid, then sat on the window seat. It was almost eight o'clock and pale orange sunlight painted the yard with a golden glow. Bridget opened her diary.

Dear Annie,

It is evening and I've endured my mother's wrath, as she told my father about my scandalous behaviour. To his credit, Father tried to keep a straight face but I could tell that beneath his stern expression, there was a smile trying to break free. I know it was wrong to embarrass Mother, but on the other hand, it was worth it to see the look of horror on Mrs. Worthington's face. As for Elizabeth, I think she pretended to be horrified to please her mother, but deep down inside, she too wanted to laugh.

Bridget turned at a knock on the door.

"Hi, kitten." Her father's tall frame filled the doorway. "May I come in?"

"Of course, Father." Bridget set down the diary.

Her father joined her on the window seat. "We have had a lot of change in our lives these last two years."

Bridget nodded.

"You must not be too hard on your mother. She only wants what she thinks is best for you."

"But she wants me to be like Elizabeth Worthington. I don't like Elizabeth."

"I agree that Elizabeth is not the kindest young lady I know," her father nodded. "However, not everything your mother wants for you is wrong."

Bridget looked up as her father continued. "She wants you to take advantage of life in Toronto. When she was growing up in Ireland, young women were not educated as you are today. And her grandparents watched friends starve in the potato famine, as did mine. Our parents came to Canada in hopes of finding a better life for their children. It is not unnatural for her to want the best for you."

"What if *I* don't think it's the best for me?" asked Bridget.

She looked out at their willow tree. A robin landed with a worm to feed her newly hatched babies.

Her father followed her gaze. "Mothers always want what they think is best for their children." He patted her shoulder and stood. "When you come to the store on Saturday you can help me unpack a new shipment of ladies' hats from France."

Bridget brightened. "Will they have feathers and lace and netting?"

"Of course. And perhaps a few sequins as well."

"I will make them into a wonderful display."

"After which we will have lunch at the Queen's Hotel on Front Street. Good night, Bridget. Sweet dreams."

After he left, Bridget sat watching the sky turn from gold to a deep orange, then hazy blue, and finally black. An owl hooted in the distance. She picked up her diary and read what she had already written. Then she began to write.

Now it's time for bed, Annie. Tomorrow I'll tell Mother that I'm sorry I embarrassed her. Then I'll practise Chopin's preludes on the piano and go to the dressmaker's to be fitted for new clothes. I'll cooperate with Mother's plans to turn me into a lady, as long as I can spend Saturdays at the store. Maybe when I'm older, I will prove that I can do both things. In the meantime, dear Annie, if "society" becomes too much of a burden, I can always sing and play my favourite Irish songs.

By the way, I forgot to mention they're my father's favourite songs, too. After all, he is the one who taught them to me. We sing them on our way to and from his store every week. "It's our music, the music of Ireland, that I want you to keep alive," he always says. And that's what I'm going to do.

Good night, dear Annie.

Your friend, Bridget.

bridget

Toronto

My New Neighbourhood:
A Young City

In 1900, my hometown, Toronto, was a thriving city and the capital of the province of Ontario. Our city had many new devices, such as electric lights and telephones and brand-new electrified streetcars.

I lived in a section known as the Annex. A very famous businessman named Timothy Eaton built a mansion there in 1889. This helped the Annex become a socially prominent neighbourhood—many wealthy people chose to live there. It was called the Annex because the area was incorporated, or "annexed," into the City of Toronto in 1883.

Timothy Eaton opened a store called Eaton's at 178 Yonge Street in 1869. He was the first merchant to introduce cash sales and fixed prices. Eaton's was the first Canadian store to offer a mail-order catalogue. It was called "The Farmers' Bible" because it allowed people in farming communities to own the same merchandise that city dwellers could buy.

This is one of our new streetcars on King Street.

Here's the Eaton's store on Yonge Street.

The Eaton's catalogue is used across the country.

In the 1800s, Toronto was a British colonial city. Even though by 1900 most residents were born in Toronto, many still traced their roots back to Britain. They felt a strong connection to the British Empire. Other ethnicities included blacks, Germans, Slavs, Scandinavians, Jewish people, and people descended from the original Natives.

Most people in Toronto followed Protestantism, but there were also many Catholics. As in Europe, there was sometimes tension between people of different religions, especially between Catholics and Protestants originally from Ireland, where my father and mother were born.

A class system developed in Toronto based on wealth and family status. Important families such as the Eatons, the Gooderhams, and the Masseys were called commercial-elite and lived in the Annex.
Next was a large middle class made up of merchants and professionals such as doctors and lawyers. Below them was a working class. The poorest people in Toronto lived in shabby shacks in the lower part of the city.

The Gooderham Mansion is one of the biggest homes in the Annex.

Hannah's Journey

Halifax, Nova Scotia, 1929

Morning

Hannah leaned over the ship's rail and watched the approaching shore. Closer and closer it came. *Canada!* How often had she said the name of her new country aloud as she walked to school or in her mind as she drifted off to sleep?

Her father was in Canada. He had gone to a city called Winnipeg a year earlier because he said there were better opportunities in Canada than in London. Now he was working as the manager of the men's clothing department in a large store called Eaton's. He said it was so large that people there just called it "the Big Store." Hannah and her mother were moving to Winnipeg to join him.

But Hannah knew that her father would not be on the pier when the ship docked. Her mother had explained that it was a long way to Winnipeg from Halifax, so he had sent them tickets for a train that they would board when they arrived. He would be waiting for them at the station in Winnipeg.

"Hannah, there you are." Her mother appeared at her side. She was wearing her plum wool coat with the fur collar and a matching hat that Mr. Watson had sent her from Eaton's. "What are you doing without your coat? You'll catch your death."

At these words, Hannah shivered. Her excitement had blinded her to the fact that in spite of her heavy wool sweater, wool skirt, and thick stockings, she was cold. Although it was March, the air still held the damp rawness of winter. She reached for the burnt orange wool coat her mother held out and eagerly put it on. It too was from her father.

"What is that place?" Hannah pointed to a row of low brick buildings rising up from the docks.

"That is Pier 21," boomed a voice behind them.

Hannah turned to find Mr. Van der Miers standing behind her. Mr. Van der Miers was a salesman for a cheese maker in Holland and travelled to Canada several times a year. "Pier 21 is the immigrant centre where you will get your papers to enter Canada." He touched the brim of his hat. "Good day and good luck to you in your new home."

Hannah jumped as the ship's horn sounded two loud blasts.

"We are docking," Mrs. Watson said. "Hannah, go to our cabin and gather your things."

The Watsons carried their valises to the pier. These were just the small bags they kept in their cabin during the voyage. Their heavier trunk luggage was already being unloaded by the baggage men from the ship to a storeroom in a building called the Annex. Mr. Van der Miers said that Hannah and her mother would go and select their luggage after they passed through immigration. The luggage was then checked by customs officers and loaded onto their train to Winnipeg. *At least I don't have to drag that heavy trunk around all by myself*, she thought.

The Watsons followed the other passengers through a set of wide doors into the building. They passed into the Assembly Hall, a large airy room filled with tables for government officials. Wooden benches for the waiting immigrants lined the floor. They found seats on a bench in the middle of the room. They were told to sit here until their names were called to meet with an immigration official.

It was a long wait. Hannah's stomach growled. She hadn't eaten anything since her breakfast of boiled eggs and toast at six o'clock this morning. To take her mind off her hunger, she studied the other passengers. Some were people she had met on the crossing. Across the aisle was the MacPherson family: Mr. and Mrs. MacPherson; their ten-year-old son, Phillip; and their thirteen-year-old daughter, Jane. They were from Scotland. They were going all the way to British Columbia, where Mr. MacPherson, an engineer, had a job with a company that built bridges.

Next to them were Mrs. Cohen and her daughter, Leah. They were also going to Winnipeg, to join Mr. Cohen. Leah's father was a greengrocer. Hannah waved and Leah waved back. The girls had become friends during the week-long sea journey. Leah wasn't happy about moving to Canada. She had spent much of the time complaining about how she would miss her friends in London and how she would hate the cold Canadian winters.

Hannah looked behind her. A family of eight filled an entire bench. They had travelled steerage class, which was below the deck. But Hannah had seen them when they came up to the promenade for walks. The mother was wrapped in a bright red shawl and wore a white kerchief on her head. Her husband wore a knitted grey vest, a long-sleeved plaid shirt, and a black hat with a wide brim. Their children were dressed in similar clothes.

They spoke a language that Hannah did not recognize. She thought, as she studied them, *I wonder where they've come from?*

"It's our turn." Mrs. Watson stood and motioned for Hannah to follow. "Come, Hannah." They walked down the aisle to the front of the room, where a man in a uniform sat at a wooden table. His name tag identified him as David Carlson.

"May I see your papers?" he asked once they were seated.

Mrs. Watson handed him their identification papers.

As he examined them, Hannah looked at the other tables. Some held two people, the immigration officer and a translator who spoke the language of the people being interviewed.

"Please, sir, how many languages do your translators speak?" she asked.

Mr. Carlson looked up. "We have people we can call on for many languages. Most of them are volunteers who were immigrants themselves. When we can't find someone, we officers must communicate the best we can, often with hand signals." He smiled. "Everything is in order, Mrs. Watson." He stamped their papers *Landed Immigrant*.

"Welcome to Canada."

Afternoon

It was after one o'clock when Hannah and her mother finally emerged from the immigration building. The sun had broken through the morning fog. Gulls screeched overhead and a ship's horn sounded from the harbour. They went to the storage room and retrieved their luggage. Then they crossed an overhead walkway into the annex where they changed their money into Canadian dollars. Next, Mrs. Watson went to the Canadian National Telegraph window and sent her husband a telegram telling him when they would arrive in Winnipeg. All that remained was for them to walk the short distance to the train.

The train tracks, which ran between the main Pier 21 building and the platform, were encrusted with soot from the steam engines. Hannah brushed dark flakes, like black snow, from her coat. As they prepared to board, a young woman came up to them and handed Hannah and her mother each a cloth bag.

"What is this?" Hannah asked.

"We call them 'dittybags,'" the woman said. "They are filled with things you can use on your journey."

Hannah looked inside. "I don't smoke," she laughed, holding up a package of cigarettes. She examined the rest of the contents. There was a cake of soap, jelly powder, razor blades, a toothbrush, a baby bottle, and a box of something she did not recognize.

"*Corn flakes,*" Hannah read. "What are they?"

"People eat them for breakfast," the woman replied.

Hannah wrinkled her nose.

"Thank you," said Mrs. Watson.

"Do I have to eat this?" Hannah asked her mother in a hushed voice. She noticed the crunchy cereal flakes scattered over the ground. "I guess other people don't know what to do with them either."

The lady heard her and smiled. "Use what you can and give the rest away. Have a good trip." The woman walked over to the next family, and the Watsons boarded the train.

Inside, the railway car had wooden seats separated by a narrow aisle. A porter in a white coat and dark trousers introduced himself as Charlie before showing Hannah and her mother to their seats. "We call this a 'colonist' car," he said, "because so many new immigrants use it."

Hannah looked at Charlie in fascination. She had never seen a black person before, although she had read about them in books. She thought he was quite handsome, with his white jacket and gleaming dark skin.

Before boarding, her mother had spent six dollars for two "outfits" that she had bought from the railway agent. Each included a mattress, curtains, and a pillow that they would use to sleep. But how these hard wooden seats would become beds was a mystery to Hannah. When she asked Charlie, he winked.

"You just wait. Tonight I will show you an amazing trick."

"What kind of trick?"

"I will turn your seats into beds."

"How?" Hannah asked, squinting her eyes.

"Well, miss, you will just have to wait and see." Charlie grinned and touched his fingers to his cap. "You ladies let me know if you need anything." He moved up the aisle to help another passenger, and Hannah and her mother sat down.

Hannah took the window seat and pressed her nose to the glass. The train's engine blasted a whistle and the train chugged out of the station. After the long ocean crossing, it was nice to see land. Hannah sat back and watched the countryside slide past. She saw farmhouses, barns, trees, and bare fields waiting for the spring planting. Now and then a farmer would wave as the train passed. Hannah always waved back.

Once the train had been in motion for a while and people were settled, Hannah looked around for Leah. She saw her sitting at the back of their car. While her mother unpacked sandwiches for a late lunch, Hannah walked down the aisle. At Pier 21 her legs had felt wobbly, as if she were still on the ship. Now she had to adapt to the rocking motion of the train. To keep from falling, she grasped the edges of the seats as she passed. *Will I ever be able to walk without bouncing?* The thought made her giggle.

"What are you laughing about?" Leah looked up from the book she was reading.

"Walking. It seems strange to be on the train after the ship."

"That's why I'm sitting." Leah patted the seat beside her. "Mother's in the kitchen preparing our lunch. Keep me company."

Hannah sat beside her. "Well, we're finally in Canada. Are you excited yet?"

"I want to see my father." Leah sighed. "But I will miss my friends and my aunts and uncles and cousins in England. What about you?"

Hannah looked out the window. They were crossing a river and she saw dots of white floating on top of the water. "There is still ice on the river," she said quietly, almost amazed.

"Canada is such a cold country." Leah shivered. "Papa says there is a lot of snow." She paused. "I haven't seen him for almost two years. I hope we will still know each other."

"Of course you'll know him." Hannah brightened, twisting in her seat. "My father says that Winnipeg is a big city with lots of exciting things to do and see."

"Hello, Hannah." Mrs. Cohen appeared holding two plates of boiled eggs and potatoes. She handed one to Leah and looked at Hannah. "Your mother wants you to go back to your seat to eat."

Hannah stood. "I'll see you later."

It hadn't occurred to Hannah to worry about the move to Winnipeg. Her father was there, and after almost a year apart, the family would finally be together. Since talking to Leah, however, she felt suddenly scared.

What if Father had changed? Would he be the same good-natured man she remembered? Or had living alone made him sour, like some of the men she had met on board the ship? The long day of travel had made her tired. Maybe she was thinking too much. After she finished eating, she leaned her head against the window and let the rocking motion of the train lull her to sleep.

Evening

Hannah awoke with a start. Something had changed. Yes, that was it: the train wasn't moving. She blinked and looked out the window into a white world. "Why have we stopped?" she asked her mother.

"There's a storm and the train tracks are covered with snow." Her mother put her hands under her arms, as if to warm them.

"It wasn't snowing when I fell asleep," Hannah said.

"These storms swirl up fast," Charlie said. He was walking up and down the aisle telling people not to worry. "The railroad crews will dig us out. Once it stops snowing," he added.

"How long will that be?" Mrs. Watson asked.

"Can't tell." Charlie shrugged. "Might be tonight or maybe tomorrow." At her worried look he shook his head. "I think we will be on our way by morning."

Hannah turned and looked at Leah. Her friend mouthed *"I told you so."* Hannah stood and walked down the aisle. "Leah, let's go outside and see the snow."

"We can't leave the train."

"Maybe Charlie will open the door and we can at least stick our heads out." She waved at Charlie.

"What can I do for you ladies?" he asked.

"We want to see the snow."

"Look out the window."

"No," said Hannah. "We want to touch it."

Charlie threw back his head and laughed. "You'll touch enough snow in Winnipeg. Now it's time to show you that trick I promised."

"Trick?" Leah looked puzzled.

"He's going to make our seats become beds," Hannah explained. She returned to her mother, who was unpacking nightgowns and toothbrushes from their valise.

"Are you ready?" Charlie asked.

Hannah nodded.

"Okay, here comes the magic." Reaching up, he pulled a top bunk down from the ceiling. Then he folded down the back of the bottom seat to form a lower berth. Mrs. Watson handed him the "outfits," and he attached the curtains to metal rods and placed the mattresses and pillows on the seats.

"I want the top bunk," Hannah said, clapping. "How do I get up there?"

"With a ladder," Charlie said.

Hannah could hardly wait to climb into the cozy bed.

Grabbing her nightclothes, she walked to the washroom at the rear of the car to get changed. Several people were lined up in front of her. One of them was Leah.

"Did you see Charlie do his magic?" she asked.

Leah nodded. "Yes. I got the top bunk. How about you?"

"Me too." She paused. "I hope I don't need to use the toilet during the night."

Leah laughed.

When they were in their nightgowns, the girls said goodnight and each went to her bunk. There was only one ladder for the entire car, so Hannah waited patiently until it was finally her turn to use it. She climbed up and then leaned over playfully. Her mother was sitting on the edge of the lower berth. "Goodnight, Mum."

"Sleep tight," her mother replied.

Hannah drew the curtain shut and snuggled down into her nest. So much had happened in one day. She had woken up on a ship, gone through the new immigration building at Pier 21, and seen Canada from the seat of a colonist car. And now she was in her own little world while a snowstorm swirled around the train and blanketed the tracks. *What an exciting start to my new life,* she thought, as she closed her eyes and drifted to sleep. 🍁

Hannah

Gateway to My Home:
Immigrants at Pier 21

When Pier 21 opened on March 8, 1928, it became a brand-new site for immigrants crossing the Atlantic Ocean into Canada. Before then, immigrants like my father landed at other locations, including other Halifax piers and ports in Montréal and Québec City. They came to Canada seeking new lives and opportunities—some to escape poverty, others because of political or religious persecution.

I was amazed how many people at Pier 21 were helping the new arrivals. Volunteers worked with immigration officials to translate for immigrants. Red Cross volunteers looked after babies in the nursery while their parents were busy with officials.

I also saw groups such as the Jewish Immigrant Aid Society and Sisters of Service helping the immigrants change money, buy tickets, and prepare for their train trips to their final destinations. On the second floor of Shed 21, there was even a dining room, hospital, nursery, and dormitories.

This is what it looked like when I first arrived at Pier 21—the start of my new life!

New immigrants all waited here to meet with customs officers.

Pier 21 was very important to World War II. This is a ship of soldiers returning from fighting overseas.

Later, during the Second World War, Pier 21 became the main port from which Canadian troops departed for Europe. Troop movements were shrouded in secrecy to prevent the Germans, whose submarines lurked just outside Canadian waters, from attacking troop ships.

When the war ended, these same ships brought the troops home. The war had also left many people displaced and homeless, and many of them found new lives in Canada. In 1956, after a revolution in Hungary, tens of thousands of people left that country. Many of them came to Canada through Pier 21.

By the time Pier 21 closed its doors in 1971, 1.5 million immigrants and Canadian military personnel had passed through its doors. I was sorry to see it close because I had such good memories of the day I arrived with my mother to begin our lives in Canada.

This is an ad for the same colonist cars that my mother and I took to get to Winnipeg.

Stepan
and the
Giant
Dust Cloud

Saskatchewan, 1935

"Mama, Mama, come outside! Come quick!"

Stepan dashed through the door and skidded to a stop in front of his mother. He had been in the yard feeding the chickens when he'd noticed a dark cloud moving toward the farm.

Mrs. Laba turned from the sink where she was washing the breakfast dishes. "Stepan, how many times have I told you not to run in the house?" She wiped her hands on her apron. "One of these days you are going to hurt yourself."

"But, Mom, there's something outside you've gotta see." Stepan grabbed her hand and pulled her out the back door. "Look." He pointed to the western sky. "See that cloud? It's going to rain." He jumped up and down, clapping his hands. "It's going to rain, Mama. It's going to rain."

His mother looked at him and for a moment a smile spread across her face. "Rain." She said the word like a prayer.

Stepan stared at the sky with his mother. He was twelve years old and could barely recall a time when it had rained enough for the moisture to sink into the ground. As long as he could remember the land on his family's farm had been parched and dry.

"Rain," his mother repeated. Suddenly her expression changed. "That's not rain, it's... Stepan, get indoors. Quick!"

She grabbed his arm and pulled him along as they raced for the house. Once inside, she slammed the door and ran around shutting windows.

"I forgot Mushka," Stepan said, confused as to what exactly was happening. He headed for the front door to look for the family's dog.

"Mushka will be fine! Sheep dogs can take care of themselves." His mother gave him a shove. "Close the windows and then get into the storeroom."

"But, Mom..."

"No buts, young man. Do as I say. Now!"

Reluctantly, Stepan closed the door. He raced into his bedroom and shut the windows, then he did the same in his sister Oksana's room. He had barely finished when the storm hit.

Stepan and his mother huddled in the storeroom of the farmhouse, away from flying glass and other debris. The roaring cloud that was sweeping over them had sucked the oxygen out of the air. Stepan thought he would choke. He covered his mouth and nose with a handkerchief; his mother did the same.

"What is it?" he whispered when the howling wind had calmed down enough so they could speak.

"Soil." His mother sighed. "It is the topsoil from thousands of farms blowing away."

Stepan looked at her, still confused. "I don't understand."

"It's nature playing havoc with us," his mother said. "We haven't had rain these past five years, so everything is as dry as dead bones. When a strong wind comes along, it picks up the dead soil. That's what's raining down on us. It's not the water we so desperately need, but acres and acres of dead soil."

Stepan brought his knees up to his chin and rested his head against them. He closed his eyes and tried to pretend that the sound he was hearing was raindrops beating against the roof. But it didn't work. He was beginning to believe that it would never rain again.

"I think it's stopped." His mother lifted her head and then motioned for him to stay where he was while she checked to see if the storm was over. Stepan waited a minute, listening to the floorboards above creaking under his mother's feet. Slowly, he too crept out of the storeroom to join her at the living-room window.

The cloud was gone but the sky and the land were grey. A thick layer of soil covered everything in sight. He tried to open the front door, but it was blocked by a wall of dirt. Walking back to the window, he hoisted it open and climbed out. As he dropped to the ground, he sank into the sand up to his ankles.

Stepan went into the barn. The dust had sifted through cracks in the boards and covered everything in a thick layer of dirt. Mossie, the family's cow, looked at him through the grimy crust that had formed around her eyes. Stepan turned to the stall where Anya, Mossie's calf, lay almost unrecognizable on a bed of hay.

Stepan sighed. This dust storm was only the latest in a series of disasters that had struck the Laba family. Like most farm families in Saskatchewan, they were on the verge of financial ruin. At night, when his parents thought he was asleep, he heard them talk about what to do when the bank foreclosed on the farm. It had been several years since they had grown a decent crop of wheat. And now his father had left home to work at a factory in Toronto. Stepan's older sister, Oksana, had gone with him and was working in a dress shop. They hoped the money they earned would save the farm from bankruptcy.

After seeing to the cows, Stepan went outside to look for the chickens. Several lay dead under mounds of dirt, but some had survived the storm. Stepan rounded them up and shooed them into the chicken coop, which, by some miracle, was still standing. Once the chickens were safe, he looked around the yard.

Fence posts had been knocked over, and wires were down. Large boards from the roof of the barn lay strewn across the yard. His mother's vegetable garden, which she had so lovingly managed to keep alive, was a flattened mess of broken stems, upended roots, and squashed tomatoes.

Suddenly, Stepan stiffened. Mushka. Where was Mushka? Their dog was nowhere in sight.

"Mushka!" Stepan called. He searched the area around the barn, and behind the house, and even peered into that cold, dark space beneath the farmhouse the dog loved. No Mushka. Stepan ran into the fields. No dog. He looked around the devastated land. When he was little, he used to love playing hide-and-seek with Oksana between the rows of golden wheat. He turned and looked at the field where the wheat had once thrived. Gold had now turned to grey, and ash-like dust covered everything. If he didn't know better, he would think those gleaming yellow crops had been burned to the ground.

Afternoon

"Never seen anything like it." Mr. Fedorko pushed his straw hat back on his head and scratched his scalp. Leaning on his shovel, he looked out over his devastated farm. "Your papa had the right idea going to Toronto," he said. "Guess you and your mama'll be joining him there soon enough."

"Mama says not while she's still breathing."

"Well, one more of these crop dusters and she might not be. Breathing, that is." Mr. Fedorko dug up a shovel full of dirt and tossed it on a pile at the side of the road. "I find myself thinking maybe I wasn't so smart to leave Ukraine after all. It may be bad there but it is no better here."

"I was born on our farm." Stepan folded his arms across his chest. "My grandfather came here from Ukraine so he could own land. He farmed it and built it up, and now Mama and Papa own it. Mama says she'll never leave."

"She may not have a choice." Mr. Fedorko sighed. "I think the bank will decide that for all of us." He peered down at Stepan. "Now, what was it you wanted to ask me?"

"Have you seen Mushka?"

Mr. Fedorko shook his head. "No, Stepan. Maybe the wind got him," he said as he looked up at the fields, "like it got everything else."

By five o'clock, Stepan had been searching for Mushka for six hours. Although it was August and the Saskatchewan days were long, the sky was dark with residue from the dust cloud. Stepan was tired and hungry. He had not eaten anything since breakfast. His head ached, his eyes burned, and his feet felt like lead after dragging them through mountains of sand. When he heard his mother ring the dinner bell in front of the house, he was almost happy to turn around.

Almost, but not quite. He still had not found his dog. Having Mushka around made these trying times a lot more bearable. He really missed him.

"Mom, Mr. Fedorko says he is ready to leave his farm." Stepan sat at the table as his mother set a bowl of steaming soup in front of him. "He says the bank will take it anyway, so why should he stay."

His mother reached into her apron pocket, pulled out a handkerchief, and blew her nose. "So he will give up, too. Just like the Romanyks and the Slyvkos. One by one, they all leave their farms. But where do they go?" She threw up her hands and turned toward Stepan, her voice becoming angrier.

"To the cities so they can stand on bread lines? They think we are the only ones hit by this plague? The whole world is in a depression. The drought is everywhere in the prairies, in both Canada and the United States."

"But if the bank takes the farm away from us, Mama, what will we do?"

His mother waved her hand. "We will worry about that when it happens." She paused, sighed, and sat at the table with her son. "Now please eat and then feed the chickens, and see that our two remaining cows are still alive. At least we will have milk and eggs so we won't starve."

Evening

Stepan finished his dinner of bread and soup, and then went out to do the chores his mother asked of him. But he was also looking for Mushka. With so much of his family already gone, finding his dog felt even more important.

As he tramped over the ruined fields, his mind again went back to when he was little. His father would hoist him onto his shoulders so he could see over the golden wheat stalks. Before his father left for Toronto, he talked about what had gone wrong.

"Stepan," his father told him, "we farmers have made terrible mistakes. All these years, we've been taking nature's bounty from the ground and putting nothing back."

"What would you put back?" Stepan had asked.

"Nutrients, food for the earth." He picked up a handful of dirt. "Wheat's a dry crop. It sucks moisture out of the soil. So when the rains don't come and the wind blows hard..." He tossed the dry soil into the air. "Nature takes away that which we fail to protect."

Stepan sighed. Nature had indeed taken away their topsoil, just as his father had predicted. Had it also taken away Mushka? Had dust buried his dog as it had so much of the land?

Suddenly, it was all too much. Exhaustion and grief turned Stepan's legs to rubber and he sank to the ground. Night closed around him. Somewhere a barn owl hooted. Cows mooed their complaints into the dusty air. Mice scampered along the ground, and the wind, softer now but still steady, continued moving the dead dirt from one farmer's land to the next.

"Uh-oh." Stepan sat up with a start. While he slept the sun had set—a grainy moon now took its place in the cool night air. He shivered. Scrambling to his feet he looked toward where he thought the house should be, but no welcoming light pricked the inky darkness. *I'm in for it now*, he thought. *My mother is going to kill me this time.*

Frantically, he searched for a landmark, any familiar form that would guide him through the vastness of the dust-covered prairie. He started walking. *If I walk in a straight line*, he reasoned, *I'll come to a farmhouse, even if it's not my own.* But the more he walked, the more lost he felt. After what seemed like hours but was probably only minutes, he stood in the field and shouted.

"Help! Somebody come and get me!"

He waited for a response. Nothing. "Yoo-hoo!" he called. "Mama! Mr. Fedorko!"

He was beginning to feel panicky. He'd stayed out all night before with his 4-H group, but this was different.

"Hey, someone out there. It's me, Stepan!" Still, he was answered by silence.

Then a distant sound caught his attention. Closing his eyes, he listened as hard as he could. Was it? Yes, it was! "Mushka!"

Stepan ran toward the barking, which was now clear and loud. "Mushka!" he cried as an enormous bundle of fur leaped all over him, knocking him to the ground. A giant tongue washed dust from his face, his neck, and his arms.

Disentangling himself, Stepan stood and stared down at the dog that was yapping at his feet. "Where have you been?"

Mushka looked up at him, head cocked to one side, tail wagging, as if to say, "And who are you to ask me that?"

Stepan kneeled down and hugged the dog. "Were you caught in the storm? Where did you hide?"

As if in answer, Mushka sneezed and shook himself hard, sending a spray of dust into the air.

Stepan sneezed, too. Then he laughed. "Mushka, do you know the way back?" He pointed. "C'mon, boy. Take us home."

Mushka paused, looked around, and then raced across the field with Stepan on his heels until the two of them crashed through the farmhouse door.

"Stepan!" His mother stopped turning the crank on the telephone mounted on the kitchen wall. "I was trying to get this thing to work so I could call the Fedorkos to ask if they'd seen you. Where have you been?"

"Looking for Mushka," Stepan grinned. "And," he said, bending down and wrapping his arms around the dog's neck, "I guess Mushka was out there looking for me, too."

Hands on her hips his mother gave him a disapproving frown. "As if I don't have enough trouble without you scaring me half to death..." She sank into a chair.

Stepan walked up to her. "Mama, this farm means a lot to you, doesn't it?"

"Of course it does. It has been in our family for thirty years."

"I know these dust storms are awful and we can't grow wheat. But it will get better. I'm twelve. That's almost a man. I can help you keep things going here until the rains come. Then Papa can come home and we'll make everything just the way it used to be."

For a moment, Stepan thought his mother would cry. Her eyes filled with tears and her nose turned red. Then she reached out and wrapped him in her arms. "My little man," she said.

Stepan stepped back and looked at her. "But next time, Mama, instead of wheat, I think we should grow corn. Maybe corn will be friendlier to the soil. Or oats. What do you think of oats?"

"I think they make fine porridge," his mother laughed, her eyes still glistening.

"I'm going to find out what crops would be good for us to plant."

"That's a wonderful idea," his mother said.

Stepan lay in bed with Mushka curled up at his feet and thought about the day. He could still taste the gritty sand that had filled his world. He thought of all the farms covered with dust and then he thought again about his father's words—*Nature takes away from us that which we fail to protect.*

Stepan made a decision. He was going to study farming. He would learn what crops were good to plant and how to treat the soil so these terrible dust storms would never happen again. He would start next week, at his 4-H Club meeting, he decided as he drifted off to sleep. He would get all his friends involved, and maybe together they would figure out how to help save their families' farms. 🍁

THE DUST BOWL

Stepan

Our Lean Years:
The Dust Bowl Farmers

In the 1930s, the Canadian and American prairies were hit by many massive dust storms, just like in my story. They started to call these parts of the country the Dust Bowl.

The farmers in these areas grew lots of wheat because it was a very popular crop around the world, especially during the First World War (1914–1918). But the soil became over-used and dry. When many years of drought came in the 1930s, all the crops died and the dry soil was blown away by heavy winds. The dust covered everything!

That wasn't all. The entire world was in the Great Depression. Many banks were closing and they could not help farmers pay their mortgages. Men like my father had to leave their farms behind.

The dust storms that hit our farms looked like giant walls of soil.

Workers all over the country protested for fairer wages and better treatment.

Many farms near where I lived were abandoned.

Many people did what my father and sister did and went to big cities like Toronto to find work. But even there it was very hard for people to find jobs. The Great Depression hit the whole country really hard.

We farmers knew that growing too much wheat had helped cause the dust storms. By the time the drought ended in 1938, we had learned about crop rotation. This meant that we planted different crops each year to keep the soil healthy.

My local 4-H Club helped me get through this tough time. These clubs were started in the United States around 1900. The symbol is a four-leaf clover with an "H" on each leaf. The "H's" stand for head, hands, heart, and health. The 4-H is there to give kids like me a place to learn farming and homemaking skills. The motto is "Learn to do by doing." I learned how to raise a calf and grow crops there. I also met new friends at the 4-H Club too.

Sent Away

Vancouver, British Columbia, 1942

Morning

Lisa ran down the front walk. Would there be a letter from Mae today?

"Could this be what you're looking for?" Mr. Crawford, the mailman, stood at their box, studying Lisa's excited skip toward him. He held up a square white envelope and read aloud the address: "*Miss Lisa Rosen*. Sounds like you."

"Yes, yes." Lisa practically snatched it from his hand. "Thank you, Mr. Crawford," she said, remembering her manners. Then she ran back into the house.

"Good morning." Her mother turned from the gas range where she was scrambling eggs. "What has you so bright-eyed and bushy-tailed this morning?"

"There's a letter from Mae." Lisa grinned, waving it in the air.

"Good," her mother said, still smiling, only now her brow bent with worry. "I hope they are all well. Imagine sending a hard-working, decent family like theirs to live in a government camp in the mountains."

Mr. Rosen looked up from his newspaper. "If we were in Germany, their government would do the same to us. German Jews are being sent away every day."

"But this is Canada!" Mrs. Rosen slapped the plate of eggs on the table so hard a chip flew off the dish. "These things aren't supposed to happen *here*."

Lisa took her place at the table as her brother, Billy, bounced into the room.

We are more settled now. We don't have a school yet but they say we will get one in the fall. I brought some books with me and I read every day. I have the copy of Heidi *that you gave me for my birthday last year. Now I understand how Heidi felt, being sent away from her grandfather in the mountains to live in a strange place in the city. Only we were sent from the city to live in a strange place in the mountains.*

One thing is good: it's pretty here. The mountains are covered with snow, and in the valley there are trees and lots of birds. We kids keep busy playing outside. The boys play baseball and the girls play tag and gather wildflowers to bring home.

I think this move is hardest on my father. Mom keeps busy caring for us. She cooks with the other women in the communal kitchen, and in the afternoons they have tea and talk about things that mothers talk about, like kids and clothes. It's harder on our fathers, who are used to going to work every day. They have so little to do. My dad keeps busy fixing things that are always breaking, like the water pipes.

"Lisa?"

Lisa put down the letter. "Yes, Mom?"

"Mrs. Williams is here for your piano lesson." Her mother peered around Lisa's bedroom door. "Oh, you're reading Mae's letter. What does she say?"

Lisa stood and shook cracker crumbs from her skirt. She held out the letter.

"She says things are getting better now that it's spring." She frowned. "Mom, I still don't understand why the government sent all the Japanese families away."

Mrs. Rosen sighed, "It's the war. People do strange things when they are afraid. They see anyone different from themselves as an enemy." Her eyes filled with tears.

Lisa knew her mother was thinking about her own relatives in Germany, whom they hadn't heard from in months. She hugged her. "They'll be okay, Mom." She handed her Mae's letter. "Read this. You'll see that it's not as bad as it sounds."

Her mother took the letter and kissed Lisa's cheek. "You're a good girl, Lisa. Now run along. Mrs. Williams is waiting for you."

Evening

After dinner, the family gathered in the living room. Lisa's father sat in his brown leather armchair, the evening newspaper open on his lap. Her mother sat at one end of the sofa, knitting, while Billy lay sprawled on the rug in front of the radio, his nose buried in the latest Superman comic book.

Her father put down his paper as the radio announcer began the news.

...the Japanese have handily captured Buthidaung from the Allies, continuing their domination of the Burma front. Allied losses in the Pacific continue to rise...

Billy pushed his comic book aside. "I told you we have to be afraid of the Jap... er, the Japanese here. The government was right to get them away from the coast."

Lisa jumped up. "What do you think—that Mae is going to stand on the beach with a lantern, signalling submarines?" She walked over and kicked her brother's comic book. "You've been reading too many of these."

"And you have your head in the sand." Billy jumped up and glared at her. "You don't understand what's happening out there."

"And you are an idiot!" Lisa railed, not backing down from her brother.

"That's enough!" Mr. Rosen shouted.

"Please, stop this." Mrs. Rosen put down her knitting, walked over to the radio, and turned it off. "Sit down, all of you," she ordered.

Everyone turned. It was rare that they saw her angry—they knew enough to pay attention. She turned to her husband. "Tom, I think it's time for a family talk."

Mr. Rosen rubbed his temples. "Billy, let's start with you. Tell us why you think that our Japanese friends and neighbours have suddenly become enemy aliens."

Billy lowered his eyes. "Because we're at war with Japan."

"Do you think your friend Tony Cavello and his family should go to a camp?"

"Of course not." Billy stared at his father.

"But they are Italian, and we are also at war with Italy," his father reasoned. "Germany, too. What about your teacher, Mr. Kurtz. Should we lock him up?" Mr. Rosen sighed. "Although, given what he's been telling you, I might be tempted to."

"Dad!" Billy shook his head. "That's different. Germany's not off our coast."

"Technically no, but as I recall, U-boats have been seen off the coast of Nova Scotia. Do we lock up all the people of German descent in the Atlantic provinces?"

"Billy." Mrs. Rosen put her hand on his shoulder. "Prejudice is dangerous. It spreads like a fire and burns everything in sight. You can dislike people for what they themselves *do*, but not for what others who look like them have done."

Mr. Rosen joined them. "It's okay to be angry at the government of Japan, which started this war, but Japanese Canadians are victims of it, just as we are."

Billy looked from his mother to his father. "Dad, do you and Mom hate the Germans for what they're doing to the Jews?"

Mrs. Rosen's eyes blazed and she tried to stay composed. "I despise Hitler, but I do *not* blame Germans in Canada for what a gang of lunatics is doing miles away."

"Just think about it, Billy," Mr. Rosen said. "And now, if nobody minds, I'm going to turn the radio on and listen to the rest of the news."

Lisa was glad to hear the radio come back on. She needed to clear her head. She went up to her room, sat at her desk, and picked up Mae's letter.

One problem is the food. We must eat what they give us and it's not what we're used to. We don't get much meat or fresh fish. The women spend hours complaining that they can't cook the way they do at home. Mom and Dad have planted a small vegetable garden behind the house, so at least we'll have fresh vegetables soon.

The worst part is we don't know how long we have to stay here or where we will live when we get out. When Mom talks about it she starts to cry and Dad gets angry. But for now, all we can do is live the best we can every day. That's what we're doing.

Dan says hi to Billy. He says he wrote him a letter but Billy hasn't answered. I know they censor some of our mail, so he wants to know if Billy got it.

Write soon. I can't wait to hear from you.

Your best friend,

Mae

Lisa wondered if Dan's letter had been censored.

She imagined all the things that the government didn't want people outside the camp to know. Was her friend hungry? Was she cold? Was there anything that she, Lisa, could do to make life better for her friend?

Lisa took a sheet of writing paper, sharpened a pencil, and began to write.

Dear Mae,

It was wonderful to get your letter. I miss you every day. School just isn't the same without you sitting behind me and giggling in my ear. In fact, I haven't been in trouble with Miss Miller since you left. What fun is there in that?

I'm practising for my piano recital. The piece is Bach and it's really hard. Mrs. Williams says I need to spend more time practicing, but I hate sitting at the piano now that the weather's so nice. I'm looking forward to summer vacation. Mom and Dad have rented a house at the beach for a week in August. I want to get my lifesaving badge so I can be a junior lifeguard next summer.

She paused and read what she had written. It all sounded so dumb. But maybe that was what Mae wanted to hear—that there was still life going on outside the camp, and that if she could just hang on, she'd get back to it after the war.

I just re-read what I've written. It sounds so trivial compared to your life. I hope this stupid war ends soon and you can come home. I miss our sleepovers. I miss you.

Give my love to your mom and dad and to Dan. Billy says hi.

Lisa stopped writing. She looked at the last sentence, thought for a moment, then left her room. She crossed the hall and knocked on Billy's door.

"Yeah, what do you want?"

"I want to talk to you. Can I come in?"

"If you must."

Lisa opened the door. Billy was sitting at his desk, fiddling with his ham radio. A pair of black earphones covered his ears. He looked up and took them off.

"I'm listening for signals from ships."

"Any Japanese submarines?" Lisa asked. She sat on the edge of the bed.

"Nah. Only a fishing trawler with a busted motor."

"Billy," Lisa began, "do you really believe those things about the Takamuras?"

"Well, not about them exactly, but—"

"Or about the other Japanese people we know?"

Billy frowned.

"And Dan is still your friend, isn't he?"

"Sure." Billy's face turned red.

"Mae says he wrote you a letter."

"Yeah."

"Did you answer him?"

"No." Billy shrugged. He fidgeted with his earphones.

"Here." Lisa handed him a sheet of paper. "I'm sending Mae a letter. Why don't you write one to Dan and I'll put them in the same envelope." She smiled slyly. "That way you can save a stamp."

Billy looked up at her and winced. "What do I say to him?"

"Start with 'Hi.' You'll figure out the rest." She waited for a minute. "Billy...?"

Billy looked at Lisa and smiled. "Okay."

"Good." She stood and walked to the door. "Night, Billy."

She stepped into the hall, shut the door behind her. *Whew*, she breathed. Billy just needed a push. She went to her room, closed the door and sat at her desk. She read the last sentence of her letter. Taking up the pencil, she added a line: *p.s. I'm including Billy's letter to Dan in this envelope.*

Folding the letter to Mae, she slipped it into an envelope. She'd add Billy's letter tomorrow and seal it then. 🍁

B.C.
INTERIOR

●Vancouver

Toronto

Lisa

A Friend's Great Challenge:
Japanese Internment Camps

The men were the first to be moved. Their families hoped they would come back soon.

After Japan bombed the American naval base at Pearl Harbor in Hawaii on December 7, 1941, Canada joined in the war against Japan. Suddenly, Japanese Canadians who lived along the Pacific Coast, even some friends of mine, were seen as possible spies for Japan.

In January 1942 our government made all Japanese men between 18 and 45 years of age move out of a 160 km (100 mi.) wide "protected" zone along B.C.'s coast. These men were sent to work in road camps in the B.C. interior. By March 1942, all Japanese people had been forced from the area. They called them "enemy aliens." It didn't matter that many of them had been born in Canada and most were Canadian citizens.

Hundreds of Japanese fishing boats
were seized and never returned.

This is the camp at Lemon Creek
where Mae was held.

My friend Mae and her family could take only what they could carry.
They had to turn over the rest of their property to the government. My
parents were sure they'd get it back after the war. Instead, in 1943, the
government auctioned off everything, including Japanese peoples' homes
and businesses. They used the money to keep the internment camps running.

Mae's letters were censored, so I didn't find out until after the war how
bad the conditions really were. Families were separated and men and
women were each sent to over-crowded holding camps. Eventually, they
were shipped in railway cars to camps in the B.C. interior, where they
lived as virtual prisoners with RCMP officers guarding them. Their houses
were either wooden boards without insulation or, even worse, tents.

As the war continued, they were eventually allowed to grow vegetable
gardens and build extra rooms on their houses, so life got a little
better. At first, the B.C. government refused to pay for schools. After
about a year, the Canadian government paid for classes in the first
to tenth grades. The Roman Catholic, Anglican, and United churches
stepped in and set up the eleventh to twelfth grades.

After the war, I thought Mae and her family would come home. But
the federal government passed a law that no Japanese person could
live in British Columbia. They had to either move east of the Rocky
Mountains or be deported to Japan. Even though Japan was in terrible
shape after the war, 4,000 Japanese Canadians left to go there. The
rest of the 22,000 people who had been displaced moved elsewhere
in Canada. Mae's family moved to Toronto. With no money and few
possessions, they worked hard to build new lives.

Lan's Boat Ride

Muskoka, Ontario, 1979

Morning

It was the dream that woke her. Her brother, Quang, was crying as waves washed over them, soaking everyone in the boat. Lan's eyes snapped open.

The cottage was quiet. She was safe in bed. Lan folded back the covers and swung her feet to the floor, shivering at the chill of the early morning dew in the air. Tiptoeing across the room, she opened the bedroom door gently so the squeaky hinge wouldn't wake Karen, who was still asleep in the upper bunk.

Careful not to make a sound—she had learned to be quiet during her family's escape through the jungle—she walked outside and stood on the deck. The morning air was cool and the lake was a sheet of grey. It was still and calm, so different from the angry sea.

"It will be safe on the boat," she said into the morning air. "I have nothing to be afraid of."

When Karen had invited her to come to her family's cottage, Lan's mother was overjoyed. But Lan had hesitated. *How could her mother do without her help?* But her mother insisted she go.

"You are lucky to have a friend like Karen," she had said placing her hand on Lan's shoulder. "She will help you become a real Canadian."

She did like the Robinsons. Karen had been her first friend at school. She had helped Lan with her English and invited her home for dinner. Mrs. Robinson never fussed when Lan did not like a certain food and Karen's older brother, Rick, had helped with her math homework.

And they certainly respected Lan. The Robinsons asked her about life in Vietnam, but when she was reluctant to answer, they did not push. Mrs. Robinson was even a teacher—Lan's mother had been a teacher in Vietnam but in Canada she worked in a hospital, cleaning rooms.

"Once she learns English, perhaps she can get her license to teach here," Mrs. Robinson had said comfortingly.

"She takes English classes at night."

"It must be hard, working all day, taking care of her family, and studying at night."

"My brother and I help her," Lan offered brightly.

"I admire you," Mrs. Robinson had said.

Yes, the Robinsons were good people. And so Lan eventually accepted their invitation. Still, she had been nervous leaving her family for three days. *How could her mother do without her help?*

Once they arrived in Muskoka, the quiet beauty of the trees and the lake soothed her. However, looking at the water and riding in a boat were two different things.

On this grey morning, Lan looked at the lake and shivered from more than just the cold.

"Hi, Lan." Karen joined her. She wore the oversized Blue Jays T-shirt and blue sweat pants that she slept in and had pink flip-flops on her feet. Her hair tumbled to her shoulders in a mass of golden brown curls. Lan touched her own straight-as-a-stick black hair. The two girls could not have been more different, yet something had drawn them together from Lan's first day in Mrs. Carey's fifth-grade class.

"Today's the day!" Karen clapped her hands. "I can't wait to see Uncle Marty's new boat."

Lan turned her head. "Karen, maybe I should stay in the cottage. There will be too many people."

"Don't be silly. There's plenty of room. We'll wear life jackets. It'll be fine."

"Yes, yes, there is room for everyone. Get into the boat, fast—before the soldiers come!" The man pushed them forward.

Lan watched her mother's face. She was trying to hide her feelings from her children but Lan knew how terrified she was. The boat was overcrowded and looked as if it would tip over with the first wave. But it was their only hope of escape.

Her mother lifted two-year-old Quang to her shoulder, clasped Lan's hand and stepped on board. As the boat pushed away from the beach, shots rang out in the jungle behind them.

"Of course you're coming with us," Karen laughed. "It's going to be awesome. C'mon, Lan. Let's get dressed." She danced across the deck. With a final look back at the lake, Lan followed.

"She sure is a beauty, Marty." Mr. Robinson stood on the quay looking down at the sleek motorboat. "Bet it churns up the water."

"Sure does."

"Uncle Marty, will you take us water skiing?" Karen jumped into the boat and examined the motor attached to the back.

"Next summer," her uncle said. "We have to get the proper equipment, and I want you and Rick to take lessons first. By the way, where is Rick?"

"At scout camp. He's a junior counsellor this year." Karen looked up at her uncle. "Can we go on the boat now?"

"After lunch," said her father.

"Yeah, I'm starved," Marty remarked rubbing, his stomach. He turned and saw Lan. "Introduce me to your friend, Karen."

Karen took Lan's hand and pulled her forward. "This is Lan. She's from Vietnam."

"Pleased to meet you, Lan." Marty held out his hand and Lan took it. "So how do you like Canada?"

"I like it very much." Lan smiled shyly.

"Do you have lakes like these in Vietnam?" Marty waved at the water.

"Where I lived, only ocean." Lan stared out at the lake. Ripples of sunlight danced across its smooth surface. She forced a smile. "Lakes are better, I think. Safer."

Afternoon

Lan stepped into the cottage and, as she had when they'd arrived, marvelled at its spaciousness. The first time she had gone to Karen's home, she thought the four-bedroom house was big enough for three families. This cottage was as big as their house—*much* bigger than the Duong's cramped one-bedroom apartment. A large front room featured an open kitchen at one end, an eating area with a wooden table and eight chairs, and a living room with two overstuffed sofas. A low wooden table was piled high with board games like Monopoly, Clue, and Scrabble. A hallway led from the living room to four bedrooms and a bathroom. To Lan, it felt like a palace.

Karen was washing dishes at the sink. Lan picked up a dish towel and walked over to help. They had eaten lunch on the cottage's deck overlooking the lake. Now they were cleaning up so they could go for a boat ride. Lan's stomach clenched. She did not want to go.

"Uncle Marty's cool, isn't he?" Karen handed Lan a dish. "He's a lawyer. He's thirty and a bachelor. My mother wants to marry him off, but he says he's happy just the way he is."

"In Vietnam, his parents would hire a matchmaker to find him a wife," Lan said. "That is how my mother and father met. Then they saw a fortune teller who said their horoscopes were good together. She promised them long life." Her smile faded. "She was wrong."

"Lan." Karen set down the stack of dishes and put her hand on Lan's shoulder. "You never talk about your father."

"His name was Tuan. That means 'smart.' And he was."

"What does 'Lan' mean?"

"Orchid." Lan laughed. "I am a flower." Her smile disappeared. "Orchids were my father's favourite."

Mrs. Robinson came into the kitchen. "Leave the dishes for now, girls. I want you to pick some raspberries before you go. Then we can have them with ice cream for dessert."

She handed them each a ceramic bowl. "The bushes are full, but be careful of the prickles."

It was cool under the fir trees where the raspberry bushes grew. Lan busied herself filling her bowl with the luscious fruit. She popped a plump berry into her mouth.

"Mmm, these are yummy," Lan said, using a new word she had learned from her friend.

Karen's mouth was already stained red with raspberry juice. "Lan, I'm sorry I asked about your father. I didn't mean to upset you."

Lan hung her head. "We don't know what happened to him. Every night my mother prayed that he would return. And then we had to escape…"

"I'm sure you'll find him one day." Karen gave her a hug.

Lan knew Karen meant well—but in her heart she knew that her father was gone.

By the time they had finished eating and put away the dessert dishes, it was two o'clock. "Time for that boat ride," said Karen excitedly.

Uncle Marty stood, clapped his hands, and then pointed right at Lan with a wide grin. "Lan, you are about to have a wonderful adventure."

Lan tried to smile but her face felt frozen.

"Put on your bathing suits, girls." Mrs. Robinson made a shooing motion with her hands. "And don't forget your hats. The sun is strong this time of day."

Lan watched Marty prepare the boat. First he grabbed an armful of orange life jackets and tossed one to each of the girls and larger ones to Mr. and Mrs. Robinson. "You too, folks," he said with a grin when Mr. Robinson protested that he didn't need one. "You have to set a good example for the girls."

"Here, Lan. Let me show you how to wear it." Karen helped Lan slip her arms through the slots and then fastened the strap around her waist.

Lan giggled. "It feels silly."

"It's not so silly if you end up in the water," Marty said with a wink. Seeing Lan's horrified expression, he softened his tone. "Oh hey, don't worry. I'll make sure you stay in the boat."

"Mama, the boat is too full. We will capsize."

"No, Lan, the man says we are safe."

"But, Mama, see. The water is angry." Lan pointed to the waves that were pounding the shore. *She looked into her mother's eyes. She knew her mother shared her nervousness.*

"You come or no?" the boatman waved a stick at them. "Get in, get in," he shouted.

"Get in, Lan," Karen prodded her. "C'mon! Don't be scared. This is going to be *soooo much fun.*"

Lan clutched the side of the boat. The rocking motion was gentle, the water calm. A few white clouds drifted overhead. The bulky life jacket pressed against her chest and chin as she sat. The only waves were from the wake of a passing boat. She began to relax.

Karen slid next to her on the wooden seat. "See, I told you this would be cool."

"The water is so smooth," Lan marvelled. "It is like a giant silk cloth." Her face broke into a smile. "I think the lake is like Canada. Even if you fall in, you have a life jacket to keep you from sinking."

"Wow, Lan, that is very profound." Marty said turning toward her. "I'll have to remember that."

Mrs. Robinson reached out and squeezed Lan's hand. "The lake isn't always this smooth," she said. "But you are right. It is calmer than the ocean, and our life jackets do protect us."

Evening

Lan tilted her head and watched the orange sparks drift up to the sky. They were sitting on the beach around the stone firepit. Mr. Robinson had lit a campfire and Karen was showing Lan how to roast marshmallows on a wooden stick.

"The campfire is my favourite part of the day." Karen scraped a charred marshmallow from her stick onto a graham cracker. Then she put a piece of chocolate on top, covered that with another graham cracker, and handed it to Lan.

Lan took a bite. "Yummy, it is so good."

"They're called s'mores. You know why?"

Lan shook her head.

"Because when you eat one, you want *smore* and *smore* and *smore*." Karen laughed. "We make them in Girl Guides. You should join my troop this fall. We do all kinds of neat things like arts and crafts and parties and camping trips."

"I don't know," said Lan, thinking that Girl Guides would cost too much money.

Karen looked at her. "You are much smaller than me. You can wear my uniform from last year so you don't have to buy a new one."

"Thank you." Lan looked at Karen. Had her friend read her mind?

Mrs. Robinson stood. "Okay, bedtime, girls."

While Mr. Robinson poured water on the fire, Mrs. Robinson handed each girl a flashlight and they all walked back to the cottage. Once inside, Karen and Lan said goodnight and went to their room.

"Wasn't this a fun day?" Karen asked as she plunked herself down on her bed.

Lan sat on the opposite bed. "Yes, a very fun day." She pulled her knees to her chest and rested her chin on top of them.

"I told you the boat would be neat. You weren't really afraid, were you?"

Lan sucked in her breath. Yes, she had been frightened. But even if she tried to explain her fear to Karen, how could a girl who had lived all her life safe in Canada understand?

In spite of Lan's fear, the boat ride had been fun. And next time, she would be more relaxed.

"I was only a little afraid," she finally said to Karen. "But once we were on the boat, then I knew we were safe."

Karen fell asleep quickly, but Lan lay on her back staring at the ceiling. Pictures from the day flashed across her mind: the soft dewy morning; picking raspberries under a hot noon sun; the campfire and the boat ride.

"It is safe to open your eyes, Lan. The crossing is over. We are here now."

"Where is here?"

"This is Thailand," said the boat captain. "The soldiers will take you to the camp where you will stay for now. You are no longer my responsibility." He rubbed his hands together as if brushing off garbage.

"Mama, are we safe now? Are we safe?"

"Of course we're safe, Lan."

"I thought you were asleep," Lan answered.

"You were talking in your sleep."

"Oh."

"I'm glad you liked the boat," Karen yawned slowly. "I hope you'll come again."

Lan thought to answer, but Karen had already fallen back asleep. She was sleepy, too. She turned on her stomach and pressed her face against the pillow. *Maybe tonight*, she thought as she drifted off, *the dream would be different. Maybe tonight the water would be her friend.*

MUSKOKA

VIETNAM

Lan

Escape to Canada:
Vietnamese Refugees

I am from Vietnam. It's an Asian country in an area called Indo-China. China ruled my country for a thousand years, until Vietnam became an independent nation in the tenth century (900s). Then, in the mid-1800s, France conquered Vietnam and ruled it until 1950. After the French were expelled, the country was divided into North and South Vietnam.

North Vietnam was a Communist state and South Vietnam was non-Communist. My family lived in South Vietnam. In 1959, civil war broke out between the two states. Communist countries such as the Soviet Union supported the North and the United States supported the South. This terrible war ended on April 30, 1975, after the Americans left. The North immediately took over the South and reunited the country under Communist rule.

On the boat, we had to find shelter from the blazing sun any way we could.

My family, and many others, did not want to live under this new government. Many people were escaping by sea to neighbouring countries such as Singapore and Japan. These refugees were called "boat people." At first, only a few people tried to escape because it was very dangerous. But as things became worse in Vietnam, more and more refugees tried to leave. By 1979, 160,000 Vietnamese, about half of them boat people, had fled their country.

These boats were rickety and sometimes capsized. People were thrown into the water. Some were picked up by passing ships, but many drowned. I was terrified but my mother told me I had to be brave. When the ships arrived at neighbouring ports in Singapore, Japan, and Taiwan, the refugees were often told they could not stay.

My family was lucky. Concerned people in countries such as Canada wanted to help the boat people. In 1978, Canada's new Immigration Act was made to meet its "international legal obligation with respect to refugees and to uphold its humanitarian tradition with respect to the displaced and persecuted."

The boats were so crowded—it was wall-to-wall people everywhere!

Many refugees from Vietnam started new lives in Canada.

The government also made something called the "Indo-Chinese Designated Class." This meant that Vietnamese people like me who were unable to return home could settle in Canada. That is how we were able to come here. The government created a sponsorship program where people or organizations could sponsor refugees. Some donated money, while others brought people into their homes.

CREDITS

Care has been taken to trace ownership of copyright material contained in this book. Information enabling the publisher to rectify any reference or credit line in future editions will be welcomed.

PHOTOS AND ARCHIVAL ARTWORK: Gordan/Dreamstime.com: 3 & throughout (background); Glenbow Archives, na-659-3: 14; Glenbow Archives, na-5571-40: 15 (left); Shayne Tolman: 15 (right); National Archives of Canada/C-011224: 24; DNY59/iStockphoto: 25 (background); Galerie Walter Klinkhoff, Montreal: 25 (top); www.canadianheritage.ca ID #10119, National Archives of Canada C-17875: 25 (bottom); Canadian Illustrated News, Vol. XXV, No. 18, Pg. 276. Photo from Library and Archives Canada: 34; Canadian Illustrated News, Vol. XI, No. 12, Pg. 188. Photo from Library and Archives Canada: 35 (top); www.canadianheritage.ca ID #10206, National Archives of Canada C-11878: 35 (bottom); Library of Congress, LC-DIG-pga-00675: 44; Library of Congress, LC-USZ62-28860: 45 (top); Buxton Historical Site: 45 (bottom); Toronto Star Archives: 54, 55 (top left, bottom); T. Eaton Company: 55 (top right); Pier 21 Historical Site: 64, 65 (top); Glenbow Archives, na-1083-2: 65 (bottom); Glenbow Archives na-1831-1: 74; Glenbow Archives nc-6-12553b: 75 (top); Glenbow Archives na-2223-8: 75 (bottom); City of Vancouver Archives, CVA 1184-12, Jack Lindsay photographer: 84; Image C-05267 Royal BC Museum, BC Archives: 85 (left); Image I-60959 Royal BC Museum, BC Archives: 85 (right); Eddie Adams/AP Photo/CP Images: 94; AP Photo/CP Images: 95 (top); Multicultural History Society of Ontario: 95 (bottom)

ILLUSTRATIONS: Peter Ferguson: cover, title page, & portraits; Celeste Gagnon: 4–5, maps

ACKNOWLEDGEMENTS

Dr. Midge Ayukawa; Morgan Baillargeon, PhD, Curator of Plains Ethnology, Canadian Museum of Civilization; Tina Bates, Curator of Ontario History, Canadian Museum of Civilization; Mary Frances Coady; Lorraine Gadoury, Library and Archives Canada; Bernard Giroux; Can D. Le, Commssioner for External Affairs, Vietnamese Canadian Federation; Andrij Makuch, Research Co-ordinator, Kule Ukrainian Canadian Studies Centre; Arthur Miki, former president of the National Association of Japanese Canadians; Mong Nguyen; Shannon Prince, Buxton Museum; Steven Schwinghamer, Research Co-ordinator and Elisabeth Tower, Manager of Education Services, Pier 21 Canada's Immigration Museum

Thanks to John Crossingham and Anne Shone for their editing insights.